Project code name:
Befriend the Brit!

She'd get to know him so well that she'd be poised to strike before he could derail her plans.

Or worse, hurt her family.

She used the house phone to ring Barrett's suite.

"It's Casey. I didn't want you going to bed hungry, so I brought fish and chips." She dangled the bait.

"A bit of fish sounds spot-on. I'll be waiting at the door of the Laredo Suite to tip the porter. And, Casey, thank you for such a thoughtful gesture."

"No thanks required, Barrett. As we say at Hearth and Home, it's my pleasure to serve you."

She picked up the sack of food and headed for the elevators.

"And as they say in Texas, You ain't seen nothin' yet, pardner!"

Books by Mae Nunn

Love Inspired

Hearts in Bloom #254
*Sealed with a Kiss #293
*Amazing Love #336
*Mom in the Middle #397
*Lone Star Courtship #445

*Texas Treasures

MAE NUNN

grew up in Houston and graduated from the University
of Texas with a degree in communications. When
she fell for a transplanted Englishman who lived in
Atlanta, she hung up her Texas spurs to become a
Georgia Southern belle. Mae has been with a major
air express company for over twenty-eight years,
currently serving as a director of key accounts. When
asked how she felt about being part of the Steeple
Hill family, Mae summed her response up with one
word, "Yeeeeeha!"

Lone Star Courtship
Mae Nunn

Steeple Hill®

Published by Steeple Hill Books™

STEEPLE HILL BOOKS

Steeple Hill®

ISBN-13: 978-0-373-87481-1
ISBN-10:   0-373-87481-2

LONE STAR COURTSHIP

www.SteepleHill.com

Printed in U.S.A.

Commit to the Lord whatever you do,
and your plans will succeed.
—*Proverbs* 16:3

Lone Star Courtship is for you, Michael.

You are my best friend, the love of my life, the head of our home and the other half of my heart. Watching you grow as you walk daily with Jesus Christ is a treasure to behold and a blessing to witness. You make it all worthwhile, my darlin'.

In loving memory of
Frasier Thomas Nunn
Our precious little buddy.
We miss you.

Chapter One

Casey Hardy was bored, a dangerous state for a self-proclaimed workaholic. Growing up the last of six children, there had always been a sibling to challenge her. Being the youngest executive in the family business, there had always been a battle for recognition. Being a female in the male-oriented home improvement industry had always forced her to be one up on all the men in her professional life in order to win their respect. And now that the challenges, battles and one-upping had paid off in the form of the job she'd had in her sights for as long as she could remember, she was bored stiff.

Her brother had handed her a project positioned for success, and following his proven plan for the construction and opening of a home improvement supercenter was a no-brainer. It was also no fun. So, Casey had an additional goal in mind when she'd headed to

Galveston, Texas. She'd take advantage of their U.K. potential investor's upcoming review of the new store's progress to prove her ability to manage an international partnership. Finally, the perfect vehicle to prove to her father once and for all that she had the stuff to be the CEO of Hearth and Home when he retired.

She stood in the bed of an old truck, her palm raised to block the midday rays of Monday's sun. Even with her thick curls caught up in a clip and a soft red bandana twisted around her forehead, sweat still prickled in her scalp and drizzled down her neck. She pulled off worn leather work gloves, stuffed them into the hip pocket of her dirty jeans and focused her attention on the arrival of a newcomer.

"Who's the suit talking with Cooper?" she asked her best friend who doubled as an assistant.

Savannah glanced up from her clipboard and looked in the direction of the foreman.

"Don't know." She squinted. "He seems familiar but I don't think it's from seeing him around here. Even as nearsighted as I am I can tell he's hot stuff and I'd remember a looker like him."

The looker was expensively dressed in a dark jacket and slacks, overdone for the Gulf Coast humidity. He'd be overdone, literally, if he didn't loosen the tie and shed that blazer. Either that or fold his tall frame back into the enormous Cadillac parked beside Cooper's Wrangler.

Casey leaned from the waist, placed a hand on the truck fender and hopped to the ground. Her steel-toed work boot slipped on the powdery shale, sending her sprawling to the seat of her pants.

"And the boss lady executes another graceful dismount." Savannah snickered, extended a hand and hauled Casey upright. "When are you gonna get a pair of sneakers with some tread on the bottoms?"

"I'm not." She brushed the dust from her jeans, grateful at least for the thick pair of gloves that had cushioned her landing. "I just need to get used to these heavy boots. Cooper says I should wear them for safety but I think it builds credibility with our crew."

"Oh, yeah, those clunkers leave no doubt that you're a construction babe. Add an orange vest and you could infiltrate a highway chain gang."

"I'm going for safe and serious, not fashionable," she defended her grubby but functional work attire.

"Thanks for the news flash." Savannah's gaze swept Casey from top to toe. "I do have to admit it's an interesting contrast to your usual uniform." She referred to Casey's closet full of dark suits.

"Hey, I didn't import you all the way from Iowa so you could insult me. That's what my family is for."

"Just keeping you grounded in the facts like your sweet daddy suggested."

"I can arrange for you to be back in the corporate office conspiring with him in person, if you'd like."

"No thanks." Savannah ignored the threat. "I'm not

going home till I catch myself a Texas cowboy." She rubbed her hands together, a gleam of anticipation in her eyes.

"I hate to disappoint you but my guess is you're more likely to rope a surfer than a bull rider in Galveston."

"If he's as hot as that guy over there with Cooper, he can ride a bike on a paper route and I won't mind a bit." She raised her eyebrows and pretended to hold a cigar, Groucho-style. "Especially if he wears one of those cute little Tour de France outfits."

"Savannah Jean, you are incorrigible."

"And you have way too much starch in your drawers, which is why we've always been good for each other."

She's right, Casey admitted to herself. *If she hadn't kept me from taking myself too seriously the past fifteen years, I'd probably be in a padded cell by now.*

Some action between the men caught Casey's eye. Cooper was pointing in her direction. He waved her over, smiling in that way he did when people first found out she was managing the project instead of her brother, Guy.

"Showtime," she muttered, then headed toward her foreman. As she closed the thirty yards that separated them she began to pick up bits of conversation. The visitor had a prominent English accent.

Her pulse quickened and she slowed her pace, needing a moment to think. He had to be the U.K. investor.

Please, God, not today. Not the way I look right now, she pleaded.

It was way too early in the project. This could only mean trouble. As in the days when she and Savannah had been summoned to the principal's office in high school, she felt the hot surge of nervous sweat. She shook off the moment of trepidation and stepped up to the men's conversation.

"Mr. Cooper, see here. There must be some mistake." The Brit pointed to the papers in his hand as if that would clarify everything. "I am specifically directed to seek out Guy Hardy, not his spokesperson. There was no correction to these instructions, no mention of an alternative contact."

"Well, son, this pretty filly right here's a bona fide alternative, not a spokesperson. And I guarantee you that's no mistake. Mark my words, *everything* this lady does is intentional." Cooper winked at Casey and discreetly spit a dark stream into his paper cup.

"Casey Hardy, Hearth and Home." She ran her palm down the front thigh of her jeans before she extended it. "How can I help you?"

"Mrs. Hardy, please forgive me if I decline your handshake." He held both palms aloft for inspection. "I had a minor mishap over the weekend." The pads of his fingers and creases of his knuckles bore some angry gashes and purple bruises.

"Yeow, that must have stung." She winced at the sight.

"Believe me, it could have been much worse. Now, allow me to introduce myself—Barrett Westbrook of Westbrook Partners, Esquire. I apologize for the intrusion. However, I'm here to meet with your husband. This gentleman says Mr. Hardy is in…" The man's brow furrowed.

"Guy's up in the hill country, near Austin," Cooper reminded the visitor.

"Yes, thank you. Tell me, madam, will your husband be down from the hills in the next day or two so we can conduct business?"

Casey risked a glance at Cooper, who was hiding his grin about as successfully as a naughty boy hid a croaking bullfrog. It was obvious he was enjoying this fellow's confusion. It was also evident Cooper had done little to clear it up and possibly even added to it. While the seasoned construction manager had been a godsend, he had way too much fun messing with her at every turn. She was enjoying the smart old codger, but this situation needed damage control. She'd start by getting the visitor out of the heat before he had a stroke.

"Would you like to walk over to the lunch trailer with me? We can get a cold drink and sit in the shade while I explain." She pointed toward the mobile unit affectionately known as the roach coach.

"Thank you for the kind offer, however I must begin conducting my investigation right away, Mrs. Hardy." He studied the papers he held as if they were critical to his very survival.

"I'm a miss."

"Excuse me, madam?" He glanced up. His brows lifted, the crease between them deepened. She'd never seen confusion look so good on a man.

"I'm a miss. A miss!"

The brows relaxed. Gray eyes the color of thick evening smoke glinted with amusement and grazed her from head to heel. "Well, I'm sure you'll clean up quite nicely after a good scrubbing."

"Yeah, she is a mess all right, but what she's trying to tell you is she's a single gal."

"Oh, quite sorry," Barrett apologized, his face a mask of poorly feigned innocence.

If this beguiling Brit was to be her potential partner, closing this deal would not only be a cinch, it would be a pleasure.

"Please do accept my apology."

She fished into her pants pockets for change.

"As long as you let me buy you a Coke." Without waiting for his response she turned toward the lunch trailer.

"Better make tracks, son. That one's not likely to slow down and give you a chance to catch up."

Cooper's advice reached her ears and she picked up the pace to drive home his point.

Barrett watched the slender young woman who, despite their joke, truly was a mess as she strode across the dusty construction lot, confidence displayed in every step. Her destination appeared to be a motor coach with its awning propped open to reveal two men selling something rolled in tinfoil. As he reached her side, an aroma unlike anything he'd ever experienced tantalized his senses. His stomach made an inappropriate rumbling sound.

"Have you eaten lunch?"

"No, I haven't had anything since breakfast on the flight this morning."

"So, you just arrived?" She deposited several bills on the counter, scooped up a sackful of the lovely smelling rolls and motioned for him to carry the cold drinks.

The chilled cans were comforting against the painful gashes on his palms and the pads of his fingers. Barrett realized he was lucky it was not his throat that was left slashed and bleeding after his insane balancing act on the edge of Traitor's Gate. His out-of-character behavior only one night earlier was proof that family pressure and fickle women could send any man to the brink of disaster.

"Get away from that ledge, Westbrook, you fool!" Sigmond cried out. "You'll slip and break your aristocratic neck!"

Captivated by the Atlantic crashing on ancient rocks three hundred meters below, Barrett ignored the needless warning of his old chum. To voluntarily leap from this site known for brutal executions, a man *would* have to be a fool. And on a rational day, he would never qualify. But just as the ruined remains of King Arthur's Tintagel lay in heaps of rubble around him, the life Barrett had carefully crafted was also reduced to a wasteland.

Nine generations of Westbrook men had succeeded in every facet of the legal profession and, according to his mum, Barrett's inability to find his fit was becoming "something of an embarrassment" to the family.

"And what would it matter if I broke my neck? I am on the brink of forty with absolutely nothing to show for myself," Barrett called above the stinging wind, repeating the words his brother had passed on courtesy of their father.

"Nothing, indeed!" Sig made no effort to hide his sarcasm. "Let's examine the facts together, shall we, my friend? First, the Westbrooks' share of wealth and respect is second only to the royal family in this country. Next, you bear the dreadful misfortune of being a ringer for that rascal Hugh Grant. How you manage to bear up under the female notice is a source of amazement." He laughed, amusing only himself.

"Then there is the lovely Caroline at your side on the rare occasion when you venture forth from your Chelsea apartment for a social affair."

Barrett clenched his eyes against the stinging wind and the biting remark.

Unbeknownst to Sig, the woman had ended their relationship two days prior. Dumped Barrett via text message for a Frenchman a half-dozen years her junior. And simply because the young scoundrel had declared himself to be in love with her. A step Barrett was not even the least bit inclined to take.

"Westbrook! Are you listening to me? Step away from that cliff or I shall drag you back by the collar and put you on the plane to America myself. In fact, some time out of your comfy chair is just what you need."

Barrett spun about-face and took several unsteady strides toward Sig to see if he was joking. The squint of the man's eyes was kind, calm, but quite serious.

"A change of scenery might do you good."

"A change of scenery is a drive up to the Lake District, not hard time in the Colonies," Barrett complained.

Sig tipped his head back, his loud laughter angled at the dark clouds. "Oh, do get over your prejudice of the Yanks. It's actually called the United States now—there are fifty of them at last count and most have paved roads and indoor plumbing. You may even enjoy yourself."

"I might agree if this assignment were in New York or California. But at the lowest point in my life my family is packing me off to *Texas,* of all uncivilized places!"

Again Sigmund's laughter rang out. He was enjoying this far too much. "Mate, Texas is hardly the

Wild West anymore. The Indians are no longer hostile and the best-known cowboys are a football team in Dallas. And you're going to investigate an investment opportunity, not negotiate a peace settlement."

His old friend was correct, as always. Barrett had failed to identify his calling within the multifaceted practice, and now he was down to his last chance with their financial division. His test would be to review an international opportunity for one of the firm's most valued clients. His report would determine the future of the partnership. To protect his own future he had no option but to make a trek to the States.

Scratch States. Make that *Texas*.

"Come along before the rain starts chucking it down. We'll get curry takeaway and have a talk while you pack."

Barrett's shoulders sagged as he accepted the finality of the situation.

"Give me a minute, Sig?"

"Of course."

Barrett lifted his face to the dark, heavy clouds that hung low, blocking Tintagel from the midday sun and the splendor of the heavens. He stood in the increasing drizzle, waiting on a sign. He began to pray aloud, without a care for Sigmund, who'd discreetly turned aside.

"Lord, You've blessed me with every advantage, yet I'm a failure at all I've attempted. I'm prepared to do anything necessary to make my parents proud while

I find Your will for me, but must I leave the land I love to discover those things?"

The declaration was sucked from his mouth and flung into the ocean before him. A gale-force wind roared across the black currents, scooped up icy seawater by the bucketful and swept up the steep cliff. A torrent of stinging ocean spray splashed Barrett hard, soaking him to the marrow and dissolving the last of his doubt.

The drizzle turned to a drenching rain. A fresh blast of wind hit him full in the chest, knocking him off balance. He struggled to keep to his feet, the leather soles of his shoes slipping on the wet ground. He pitched backward, his arms thrown out in a useless effort as he tumbled hard to the seat of his trousers.

An uncontrollable slide toward the sheer cliffs caused Barrett to cast about with his hands, grasping for jutting chunks of stone that slashed his palms as he inched toward Traitor's Gate. He dug his heels into the earth, pushing with all his might. A gush of water coursed beneath him in its rush to blend with the sea. It picked up speed, swept down the slope, whooshed over Barrett and pulled at his sodden clothes, sucking him toward the ledge. Having spent countless days sailing the always-freezing water, there was no terror in Barrett at the thought of falling, of drowning. There was no fear of death, only wry irony that life could end on the cliffs of this magical place, never having found his own Camelot.

* * *

Barrett shuddered at yesterday's memory. The Heavenly Father had never taken His eyes away and neither had his friend, Sig. If ever a man had wanted a sign, that was most surely it.

The humid air of Galveston, Texas, was a warm and welcome change.

"Let's sit over here in the shade while you answer my question." Casey lifted first one heavy boot and then the other across a wooden bench, sat and motioned for him to do the same.

Having lost the thread of the conversation, he simply followed her example. "I'm sorry, what question was that?"

"I asked if you just arrived this morning." She busied herself with the contents of the sack, laying out napkins and plastic ware.

"Oh, yes. My flight from Gatwick landed in Houston just after daybreak. I rented a car and drove straight down, *Miss* Hardy." They exchanged smiles. He fancied hers. It was a lovely distraction from the memory he planned to bury forever once the telltale signs were gone from his hands. "It was my intention to introduce myself to your…" He paused, expecting her to fill in the blank.

"Brother. Guy is my big brother. He recently married and settled in Austin, and I've taken over his position as the executive of corporate expansion."

"That presents quite a different situation than I'd

been led to expect." He couldn't help wondering if his father had known about this all along. "It was my intention to make your brother's acquaintance and agree together on a brief timeline to review all necessary materials."

She stopped her work of laying out their meal and narrowed unforgettable eyes that reminded him of the bluebells in his mother's garden.

"Who did you say you were with again, Barrett?"

"Forgive me for not presenting my identification when we made introductions." He drew a slim leather case from his breast pocket and positioned a business card on the table before her.

"Westbrook Partners, Esquire. My family has provided legal representation for nine generations."

"And your family is diversifying by investing in the U.S. home improvement market?"

"Good heaven's, no," he insisted, possibly louder than necessary.

The rag the woman had twisted around her head must be too tight. He would never suggest such a thing to his family and wasn't at all sure he'd recommend the client do so, either. This mission was critical and he had no intention of failing. Again.

"Well, you don't have to make it sound like a bad thing." The tilt of her brows indicated he'd offended her.

"Please, allow me to explain. I represent the U.K. group interested in Hearth and Home. I'm here to review and report on the legal implications of moving forward."

"So, you're a financial adviser?"

"More accurately, I provide legal guidance on financial matters."

"You're a *lawyer?*"

She used the word as if it were synonymous with ax murderer.

"I'm a barrister, that's correct."

She dipped her chin, looked at the items she'd put on the table and muttered something under her breath that clearly included the phrase, "An ambulance chaser with an accent." She began to unroll one of the tinfoil objects.

He mirrored her actions with the mystery food, having no idea what to expect inside. Hopefully a hearty serving of pork pie or Cornish pasty.

"I see you have high regard for my profession," he observed, not at all offended. It seemed to be a common opinion the world over.

She raised her face, met his gaze.

"My family lost a small fortune and spent months in court thanks to money-hungry lawyers. Even so, that doesn't give me the right to be rude." A charming pout puckered her lips. "The simple truth is I'm disappointed. I was expecting your client in person."

"I'm sorry to let you down. I'll do my best to make amends." He offered up a smile, removed his suit coat and loosened the Windsor knot in his tie.

Her grin was sheepish. "Now it's my turn to apologize. I've reacted like a petulant child and that is not the first impression I usually give."

"Nonsense, you cast a lovely image, and perfectly suitable for the surroundings." He angled his head, indicating the catering coach. Her eyes widened with exaggerated offense.

He raised a sore palm to shield him from the expression. "You must admit, we've both had a bit of a shock in the past half hour. What do you say we start over?" He lifted his soft drink and offered a salute. "To new beginnings?"

The blue eyes narrowed while she considered the proposal, as though it were possible she'd refuse his toast. Then a sly smile curved what might be the most perfect mouth he'd ever seen. She raised her soda.

"To new beginnings," she agreed.

The two cans made contact with a clunk.

As they flipped the tabs of their drinks and took first sips he considered his interesting change of circumstances. The hard-driving American businessman he'd expected to find had turned out to be an attractive young woman. If her footwear was any indicator she was more concerned with work conditions than appearance. Quite a nice change from most females in his life and nothing at all like Caroline. Maybe his luck was turning about. Maybe this woman would be so involved with the nuts and bolts of construction that she'd leave him to his work.

He felt a burden lift from his heart. Yes, things were looking up. In no time at all, his task would be complete. This trial by Texas would be a thing of the past and he'd be heading home.

He remembered the quote for the day on the calendar in his office. *Keep your friends close and your enemies closer.*

He didn't yet know which she was, but either way during his stay in Galveston he'd stick close to *Miss* Casey Hardy.

Chapter Two

Casey watched with fascination as Barrett studied his tamale. His grim confusion was priceless, reminding her of the first time she'd encountered a plateful of boiled crawfish.

"What is this part?" He poked at his food with the tines of a plastic fork.

"A corn husk."

"So, swine food is to be my first meal in Texas."

"You don't eat that stuff. It's used to roll the tamale and then hold it together while it's cooking." She took pity on the guy, something she never thought she'd do with a lawyer. "Here, like this."

With practiced fingers she peeled away the moist husk to reveal the steamy contents.

"So that's how it's done." He smiled as he followed her example, but resumed his look of concern when he raised a forkful to his face and studied it.

"The meat on the inside is roasted pork and the stuff on the outside is made from Mexican cornmeal." She lifted the food with her fingers and put away the tasty Mexican staple in two unladylike bites. Her mother would raise her eyes heavenward and wonder where she'd failed, but with her kids there always seemed to be a connection between clothing and table manners. When they were casually dressed, proper behavior seemed to fly out the window.

To atone, Casey dabbed her lips daintily, wiped her fingers with a paper napkin and then motioned for her company to eat up. Barrett disposed of the initial suspicious bite then forked the rest and popped it in his mouth. He closed his eyes while he chewed as if giving all his concentration to the flavor.

"Jolly good," was his simple declaration as he motioned toward the sack. "May I have another? I'm famished."

"That's why I bought a dozen."

He reached into the brown paper bag. "I'd like to hear the details of your expansion plan. Would you mind telling me something about that while I eat?"

She glanced at the time. Cooper had arranged for their primary contractors to join her in the construction trailer at three o'clock sharp and she still had plenty to do before their meeting. Savannah was nothing if not efficient, so Casey was certain everything would be pulled together and ready when she took her place at the head of the conference table. Still, there were things she had to handle herself.

"I've caught you at a bad time, haven't I?"

The worried crinkle around his eyes gave away his anxiety over her response. She waved away his concern while she fished a cell phone from the pocket of her grubby shirt.

"No, but I do need to juggle some stuff. You enjoy your lunch, I'll step away for a few minutes to make some calls and we'll wing it from there."

In response he expertly shucked his second tamale, ate it in two bites and then mimicked the way she'd dabbed at her lips with a napkin.

No doubt his way of saying he wasn't missing a thing.

Just like a lawyer.

She glanced over her shoulder at the visitor and tried to ignore the tingling in her fingers as she rounded the flatbed trailer piled six feet high with tons of Sheetrock. Guy answered her call on the second ring.

"What's up, kiddo?"

She ducked into the truck's shadow for cover and privacy.

"What's up is there's a lawyer here to see you and it seems he came all the way from London," she snapped at her brother.

"Oh, he must be the rep from Westbrook Partners."

"You knew this guy was coming? Why didn't you

warn me?" With the first question her temples began to throb. With the second her voice crescendoed to a squeak.

"Easy, girl! You'll shatter a windshield." His chuckle buzzed in her ear.

"Don't you dare make jokes. Just answer my questions." She squeezed her cell phone, wishing she could do the same to his neck. It was so like him to test her with a surprise.

"Of course I knew he would be coming eventually but not for another month at least, so I hadn't thought to warn you about him. What does he want?" His calm and lack of excitement was the right medicine to slow her heart from the racing that had begun.

"He says he's supposed to go over our expansion plan."

"Well, cooperate with him. Let the man have what he needs and then he'll leave."

"Guy, *he's a lawyer.* We can't trust him with that kind of information."

"Casey, you can't let our experience in court make you bitter for the rest of your life."

"But that Nashville lowlife faked his injuries in our store and those lawyers not only went along with the deception, they fought tooth and nail to get that huge settlement."

"Hon, lawyers are *supposed* to trust their clients and they don't get paid if they don't win."

How her brother could be so forgiving was a

mystery. He'd suffered the most during the dragged out proceedings of the personal injury claim. But he'd given his anger to God and forgiven the people who'd made false claims. Today, he was happily married and about to adopt his wife's precious little son.

"So you've told me a hundred times," she continued, "but I'm not ready to offer wholesale absolution. In my book the entire legal community is guilty of being money hungry until proven otherwise."

"Well, reserve judgment and give this fellow the benefit of the doubt, Warden. Westbrook Partners is the most respected law firm in England. Their influence on the investor could make or break our deal."

"Okay, okay, I hear you. I won't let the family down."

"Hey, Casey?"

"Yes, Guy?"

"The last thing any of us worries about is you letting the family down. Dad hired you to replace me because you've trained for the opportunity and everybody knows you've earned it, because you keep reminding us. Call me tomorrow."

"I will. Thanks, bro."

"Now go leave your mark on Hearth and Home."

She closed her cell phone and smiled. Guy's reminder of her number-one personal goal was just the thought to get her through the afternoon.

"Yeah, I hear you and I'll do my best to follow your advice, but I'm keeping a close eye on this limey legal eagle, just in case."

* * *

Barrett's clothes were sticking to his skin. Even though he'd shed his jacket and tie and rolled up his sleeves, he'd still perspired through his undershirt. His trousers were streaked with whitish dust and his button-down looked and smelled as though he'd worn it to shear sheep.

He was hot, he was uncomfortable and he was beginning to feel the effects of two sleepless nights and jet lag. Add the unaccustomed seasoning of his gluttonous lunch and he was closing in on a sensory meltdown. Still, as much as he wanted to check into the famed Galvez Hotel, take a cool shower and fall across a king-size mattress, he wanted to make progress on this assignment more. Once he had details and a starting point, he could begin organizing his thoughts. He would treat the exercise like the writing of a graduate school research paper. The kind of work he loved. And the reward would be returning to London with a mission successfully accomplished.

Finally.

But right now he had to take his sticky, rumpled self to, of all unappealing places, a construction trailer to observe a woman in dirty work boots giving orders to her hired help. Two hours earlier she'd excused herself and left him in the company of her man Cooper for a tour of the site. While it had been an enlightening use of his time, Barrett's gut told him the gangly old guy was a decoy. In fact, he had the distinct feeling the aging foreman was stalling for his employer. As he aimed disgusting spittle into a paper cup, Cooper was forthcoming enough on matters related to construction but questions beyond that were deflected with shrugs and feigned ignorance. The old boy was about as ignorant as a Scotland Yard detective. Years of Oxford-trained cross-examination skills were essentially wasted on this Cooper fellow.

At the end of the tour Barrett was given directions to the meeting place. He parked his luxury sedan alongside several ostentatious pickup trucks and entered a building that was nicely, if temporarily, constructed.

A blast of cool, dry air greeted him as he stepped inside. Barrett noted the professional decor of the interior, dimly and comfortably lit in contrast to the glaring afternoon sun. For a moment he battled the desire to locate and stand beneath the air-conditioning vent directing the chilly breeze down the neck of his unbuttoned dress shirt.

"Good afternoon, Mr. Westbrook."

A smiling creature crossed the room.

"I'm Casey's personal assistant, Savannah, and I've been warned about your injuries so I won't offer to shake hands. May I at least get you some tea?"

"That would be lovely. Yes, please. And do call me Barrett."

"I'll just be a moment, Barrett. There's a powder room through there if you'd like to freshen up."

The curvy brunette in jeans and sneakers gave him a cheeky smile, made a tick mark on the clipboard she carried and turned to leave.

He seized the opportunity to duck into the small room where he washed his battered hands and splashed cool water on his face. As he stood before a large decorative mirror, he reviewed the day's damage. Dark smudges beneath his eyes, hair askew, clothes limp and wrinkled. He looked as disheveled as he felt. A strong cup of Earl Grey with lemon would help him endure the afternoon. He considered going out to the car for his jacket and tie, but hadn't the energy.

"When in Rome," he reminded himself of his best friend Sig's advice to blend in rather than stand out. So far everybody he'd encountered was in laborer's attire so there was no need to drag back on the wool jacket that had been so appropriate twenty-four hours ago in fog-dampened London.

Back in the reception area he stepped close to a wall of framed photos that seemed to chronicle the growth of the company. Interspersed with aerial shots of the huge stores were smiling faces of employees at various gatherings. Casey's eyes flashed at him from several of the pictures as she stood arm in arm with people who resembled her too much to be anything but family members. They appeared to be a large and cheerful lot.

"Barrett, if you'd like to join them, the other men are waiting for Casey in the conference room." The assistant motioned toward the double doors at the end of the reception area.

"Super," he agreed.

She went before him and pulled one of the doors wide. It was immediately clear his lack of more professional attire was a blunder. Three men were grouped together at the far side of the room, impeccably dressed in summer-weight suits and gleaming leather cowboy boots. Three wide-brimmed straw hats hung behind them on a rack made of some deceased animal's antlers.

"Gentlemen, this is Barrett Westbrook of Westbrook Partners, Esquire." Savannah made the introductions. "Barrett, may I present Doc Mosley, George Duncan and Manny Fernandez. Keep an eye on your wallet around these three. They're known as the Cowboy Cartel and they'll make a partner out of you quicker than you can sing 'The Eyes of Texas.'"

"Well done, little lady." The man identified as George winked at Savannah, a woman less than half his age. "Nice to meet ya, Westbrook. Put 'er there." He thrust out a tanned and weathered hand.

Barrett extended his palm upward but before he could explain his injuries George had him locked in a grip that nearly induced tears. Doc stepped forward next and clasped with equal fervor. By the time Manny ended his bone-crushing assault, Barrett's hand was numb. He gently flexed his fingers and slipped his right hand into his trouser pocket, determined not to check for bleeding.

"Would you like lemon in your tea, Barrett?" Savannah stood at a sideboard with her back to the men.

"Yes, please. And milk if you have it."

Her dark head turned as she lifted a glass filled with ice and amber liquid. "It's cold tea and it's already sweet. I hope that's okay since it's the only way to drink it here in Texas."

"Yes, of course. Even better after such a warm day."

"Yeah, doggie." Doc slapped a beefy hand on Barrett's shoulder. "You can't ask for nicer weather than this. Bet the water's eighty in the bay today."

Barrett's concern for his hand abated. "Eighty degrees Fahrenheit?" That was a Roman bath compared to the ocean temperature back home. He had to find a marina where he could rent a sailboat. Suddenly a short stay in Texas held some appeal.

"Marine report said eighty-one." Manny nodded. "Perfect for specks. You fish, Westbrook?"

"Not since I was a youngster on holiday with the family. My grandpa fancied a bit of wading with a surf rod. I myself am partial to a sail over an outboard motor."

"How 'bout joining us anyway?" Manny extended the invitation. "We're making a run out to Trinity Bay. I'll put you on a mess of trout. What do ya say?"

Barrett glanced toward Casey's assistant who waved away his question before he voiced it.

"Casey's booked solid in the morning. She can't possibly see you before lunch anyway. Go enjoy yourself."

Barrett would much rather skim over the waves than dangle a hook beneath them but it would be inhospitable to reject the kind invitation. Besides, he might discover something of value from these chaps.

"If you're sure it's not an imposition, I accept." Barrett nodded. "It's very generous of you to offer."

Doc began to make a sound that Barrett could only surmise was laughter. The man displayed all of his teeth and tossed his head, not unlike a braying donkey. The odd sound was infectious and Barrett felt a smile pulling at his mouth though he had no earthly idea why.

"What does your friend find so amusing?" he had to ask.

George spoke up. "The idea of Moneybags Manny being generous is something to laugh about all right."

"Hey, wait a minute now." Manny pretended to be offended.

"Save it for the company, dubs." George waved away Manny's objection. "There's not a charitable bone in your body, and you know it. You still have ninety cents of the first dollar you ever made and I've watched you pinch a penny hard enough to make Lincoln yelp."

"Westbrook, this old cuss is just inviting you along so he'll have a chance to outfish somebody for a change." Doc elbowed Manny in the ribs.

"Well, there may be some truth to that." Manny's eyes glinted. "At the very least you're in for a nice boat ride in the morning."

Barrett nodded, sensing that more was in store for him than a boat ride.

"I see you gentlemen have been introduced."

All heads turned toward the soft voice. The lovely creature gliding toward them in a chic navy suit, crisp ivory blouse and snakeskin pumps was a stranger.

Or was she?

"That's a fact, Miss Casey," George answered for the group. "And you left us alone just long enough for Manny to scare up a fishin' trip."

"Imagine my surprise." When the dark-haired beauty smiled, turning azure-blue eyes on Barrett, he was no longer uncertain of the newcomer's identity. Casey Hardy definitely responded well to a good scrubbing. She was stunning.

"Barrett, we're pleased you could join us today. Shall we get right to work?"

She took her seat at the head of the small conference table. The men flanked her on both sides and Savannah sat at her right, tapping on a laptop keyboard.

While Casey and her contractors conducted business, Barrett listened and sipped tea sweet enough to make his teeth ache. To Casey's credit, the meeting was to the point and efficient. She was clearly in charge, insisting on corrective action when a quality concern was brought to her attention. The men showed the young woman sincere respect and when the meeting adjourned each packed his attaché case with a list of directives from Casey Hardy.

"Where you stayin', Westbrook?" Manny was organizing the next morning's trip and it now seemed Doc and George would accompany them. "We'll pick you up. Four a.m. okay?"

Barrett did the math. His body clock was set seven hours ahead and he had no intention of being around long enough for that to change.

"I shall be ready and waiting at the front door of the Galvez."

"Nice old place." Doc nodded his approval. "But if you're going to be here more than a few days we need to break you out of there and set you up in one of our condo units on Tiki Island."

"Oh, that won't be necessary." Barrett was adamant.

"Suit yourself." The men left their contact cards, donned the matching cowboy hats and stepped out into the humidity.

Casey stood and gathered her notes.

"I realize it's been a long day for you, Barrett, but if you wouldn't mind, I'd like to hear your objectives for this visit."

Before he could answer, a phone began to ring in the next room.

"I'll get that, Savannah." Casey tucked pages into a leather binder. "Will you join me in my office, please?" The phone rang again and she dashed from the conference room, evidently certain he would comply.

"Better hurry, she won't wait on you to catch up."

"That's the second time I've been told that today."

Savannah grinned. "Welcome to the orbit of Casey Hardy. She spins fast and you're either pulled in by her gravity or slung out into space. Either way, it's a wild ride."

Barrett stepped into the office with Casey's nameplate on the door. She was already on her cell phone, a small pair of tortoiseshell glasses low on her nose as she referred to a spreadsheet before her. She gave him an apologetic smile and held up her index finger, indicating she'd only be a minute.

Unlike the well-appointed and spacious conference room, this work area was small. The desk and credenza were piled high with files. A desktop as well as a laptop were booted up within arm's reach, appointment reminders flashing on both monitors.

"Organized clutter," he noted, and couldn't help wondering if that was the way her mind operated.

A whiteboard covered with brightly colored Post-it notes hung at eye level to the left of the desk. He was delighted to find the handwritten words were quotes. Being a fan of a well-turned phrase, he'd always had an appreciation for words of wisdom that stood the test of time. Right in the middle of the board was a phrase that caught his attention and almost took his breath.

Keep your friends close and your enemies closer.

Chapter Three

Casey replaced the handset without a sound and returned her attention to the strikingly handsome man in her office. Rumpled and wrinkled and with a lock of hair drooping over his forehead, he was dangerously appealing. His shirt gaped open at the throat, revealing a flash of tanned chest that matched the sun on his face. An outdoorsman.

Probably a golfer. She'd always wondered at the intelligence of those who wasted their time and money chasing a dimpled ball with a metal club and called it sport. Yep, she'd bet he was a golfer.

He stared at her Post-its.

"My moments of Zen," she explained.

"Zen?"

"You know, contemplation and meditation."

He grinned at something he read, his profile alight

with humor, deep with character. Her insides squirmed in the most delightful way.

"Is that why you collect them?"

"Not really, but it's one of the nice benefits of the effort."

He read out loud. "'A mountain lion roared with pride after he'd eaten a longhorn steer. He made so much noise that a hunter shot him. Moral—when you're full of bull, keep your mouth shut.'" He turned puzzled eyes to her. "I don't quite get that one."

"Hang around Texas for a while and you will."

"In that case you'd better explain it to me now, as I have no intention of being here long enough to decipher colloquialisms."

He won't be around long. Hot dog!

Her heart thumped with relief. Then, just as quickly, it wilted with regret.

He won't be around long. What a shame.

"So, your visit will be a short one?"

"That depends upon you, actually."

He dropped into one of the visitor's chairs, propped his leather case on his knees, ran his thumb across the combination lock several times and popped the lid open.

"I have a list of queries." He lifted a handful of documents. "Until all are addressed satisfactorily, I will be underfoot, but not a moment longer."

She leaned toward him, held out her hand and offered just the smallest smile.

"May I?" She used her most persuasive voice.

Seemingly unaffected, he shoved the pages beneath the lid, closed it and spun the lock.

"I'm afraid I cannot release those documents without written authority from my client."

"And Savannah says I have starch in my shorts," she muttered.

"Hmm…" He narrowed gray eyes and pretended to think. "If I'm interpreting correctly, you are saying my stiff demeanor may be induced by my undergarments. An interesting if uncomfortable visualization."

She struggled to hold back a grin. He caught on quick.

"I meant no offense," she apologized. Sort of.

"None taken. But I must observe company policy."

She imitated his accent.

"Come now, Barrett. Surely it won't break rule number one to share the subject of your queries?" Her pitiful effort probably resembled a chimney sweep more than the Queen Mum.

His eyes flashed and a wry smile curved very inviting lips. She couldn't wait to share the news of this unexpected hottie with the four older sisters who constantly worried about Casey's complete lack of a personal life.

"Jolly good cockney you've got there."

"Thanks, that's just what I was going for," she lied.

One dark eye blinked so quickly it was impossible to tell if it was intentional.

Was he flirting? Her heart thumped.

Casey Hardy, get a grip. You are thirty, not exactly desperate. Yet. And this guy is a lawyer, for crying out loud. A wolf in sheep's clothing however sharply dressed.

She gave herself a mental shake, uncrossed smooth bare legs beneath the desk and sat taller in her chair.

"All joking aside, tell me how I can cooperate. And I'll make it my personal mission to get you on the next flight back to Merry Old England."

Barrett flinched as if a stab of pain accompanied her comment. This woman was obviously anxious to be rid of him. Was this becoming a pattern in his life?

Casey leaned closer, her dazzling blue eyes filled with concern.

"Are you okay?" She'd noticed his discomfort.

"Yes, of course." He looked down at his wounded palms, seized them as an excuse. "It's just these scrapes. They're fairly fresh and a bit painful still."

"Here, let me get my first-aid kit." She tugged a knob on her desk and began riffling through what was inside the deep drawer.

"That's not necessary, really," he tried to assure her.

"Oh, don't be a martyr. A couple of those cuts look pretty deep. The least you can do is put some ointment and a Band-Aid on them. I'm sure I've got some in here somewhere."

As she continued to poke through the jumbled contents, Barrett stole a close look at Miss Casey

Hardy. She was a vision in cream and navy. Her springy dark curls fell across clear skin colored by the sun and a sprinkling of freckles. She wore only enough makeup to darken her lashes and add an inviting hue to the lips she puckered in concentration.

"Ah-hah!" She held a small tube and several wrapped plasters aloft. "Now, let's see those hands."

Before he could object she rounded the desk and stooped to get a good look at his injuries.

"My siblings don't call me the Warden for nothing. Now, do as you're told and you might get time off for good behavior."

He let go a sigh of resignation and offered first one palm then the other. Her fingers were cool and gentle as she dabbed salve on the jagged lacerations, covering several with small strips decorated by brightly colored fishes.

As she applied the third plaster her incredible gaze met his. A spark of mischief lit her eyes.

"I hope you don't mind Nemo and Dory. I keep these cute Band-Aids handy for my eleven nieces and nephews. There always seems to be a little one bouncing off the sidewalk."

"Sounds like you have a large family." Her touch was kind. It was easy to imagine her ministering to children.

"I'm the youngest of six. Since my brother and four sisters all have kids, I try to keep candy and first-aid supplies at hand." She smoothed on the last dab, replaced the cap, tossed the tube on her desk and reached for a tissue.

"All done," she announced as she cleaned her hands. "How about a lollipop while you tell me what you need and when you plan to be on your way."

He resisted the urge to cringe again. Having a beautiful woman barely masking her desire to be rid of him really was a shot to the ego, especially given his recent romantic dismissal.

"If we could begin with the financials tomorrow and work through your business plan over the next day or so, I can easily make my flight on Friday."

"Outstanding."

She slapped her hands together and rubbed them as if his departure was a source of great anticipation. Then she stood and moved toward the door, signaling his company was no longer desired. If he didn't make an exit soon, his self-confidence would be as battered as his palms. A cool shower, a cup of steaming chamomile and a few mindless minutes of public telly would wash away the day's events so he could sleep.

"Yes, indeed." He pushed to his feet and lifted his attaché, pausing for her to proceed first.

As she placed one very high heel before the other, it was impossible not to admire the woman. Though she was a vision of corporate life in dark navy, the expertly tailored suit was all female. The fashionably flared hem of her narrow skirt whisked the backs of her bare knees, drawing his eyes to firm calves and slender ankles.

"Oh!" Her head turned with a sharp snap, too quick for him to pretend he hadn't been admiring her legs. Her lips curved at the corners. "Would you like company for dinner?"

Barrett warmed at the touch of her smile but knew it was nothing personal. Women naturally enjoyed male attention, didn't they? Caroline certainly had. In fact she'd regularly reminded him it was her mission to catch the eye of every man in the room during social evenings. She relished the events while he attended the dreadful dinners only out of obligation and her insistence.

Another aggravation he wouldn't miss. Sigmund had pointed out the breakup was probably a blessing in disguise. Maybe he'd been on to something.

"Barrett?"

He dismissed the train of thought and focused on the vision before him.

"Dinner, yes, of course."

"What time would you like to eat?"

"I mean, no!" he blurted.

Her eyes widened.

"My apologies. What I meant to say was yes, thank you, but no, thank you. My unusual lunch will be with me for hours yet, so you don't need to go to any trouble or change your plans for me."

Her eyes glinted then narrowed as if amused. She lowered her chin to look at him over the rim of her glasses. She graced him with a fetching flash of blue through thick sable lashes.

"Actually, Cooper offered to carry you out for a steak. I can't afford to take the evening off myself."

"Well, there you have it then." He backed toward the exit, feeling a fool for his assumption. "Makes sense you wouldn't want to be caught dining with the likes of a barrister."

"On the contrary, I eat with tax collectors and lepers regularly." Her lips parted, flashing a white smile.

He grasped an imaginary dagger, pulled it from his chest with a soft "Ugh!" and offered it to her. "You should keep this for yourself. You'll need it to carve your budget figures after we review the finances tomorrow. Cheers, *Miss* Hardy." He turned toward the door, feeling fortunate to be leaving with the last word said.

"Oh, Mr. Westbrook?"

"Yes?"

"When you're full of bull it's best to keep your mouth shut."

"Ahhhhhhhh…" He tapped his index finger to his temple and nodded. "Now I get it."

Casey stood in the lobby of the Galvez Hotel and marveled over the turn-of-the-century opulence while she waited for Captain Jack's delivery vehicle. She checked her wristwatch: 9:00 p.m. She should have called first, but it was on the way home and Captain Jack's made the best fish and chips south of Keokuk, Iowa. Bringing Barrett something to eat was simply spur-of-the-moment Southern hospitality. At least, she hoped he'd believe that story.

From the moment she'd peeked through her window shade to watch his huge Cadillac cross the dusty construction site, the seed of a plan had begun to germinate. Her background in corporate quality told her it was too quickly conceived. But Father Time was like the girl in high school who'd tried to convince Casey a perm would actually *straighten* her hair.

The enemy!

She didn't have the luxury of plotting carefully and applying Six Sigma analysis to find the defects in her plans. Instead she'd keep copious notes and review her progress each day as she moved aggressively toward her goal.

Project code name: Befriend the Brit!

Okay, so it was about as firm as a soup sandwich, but she'd made worse conceived notions work before. This would be a snap.

She'd drive him nuts with questions and develop a fascination for all things English that made her mistrust of the legal profession no longer seem relevant. She'd get to know him so well that she'd be poised to strike before he could derail her plans.

Or worse, hurt her family.

And then there was the side benefit of spending a few days with a man who was very easy on the eye. That would help turn this bitter pill into a jelly bean.

"Ma'am, is that the delivery you were expecting?"

The bellman gestured toward the hotel's circular drive. A mustard-yellow van bearing the likeness of a pirate waited with emergency lights flashing.

She paid the driver, carried the warm bag to the front counter and used the house phone to ring Barrett's suite.

"Yes, h'lo?" His voice was raspy.

"Were you asleep, Barrett?"

"It's…" There was a brief pause. "Four a.m. Of course I was asleep. Who is this?"

"It's Casey. I'm so sorry to wake you. I didn't consider the time difference."

In truth, she knew his body was on London time, seven hours ahead. Step one of her plan was to catch him unprepared, get a glimpse of his true nature.

"I've come bearing gifts."

"Gifts? At this unearthly hour?"

She smiled at the crescendo of disbelief in his voice.

"This unearthly hour is only 9:00 p.m. I didn't want you going to bed hungry so I brought fish and chips." She dangled the bait.

"Ale-battered?" The Brit nibbled.

"Probably." She had no idea.

"With malt vinegar?"

"Of course!" Picky, picky.

"Cod or haddock?"

"I don't knoooooow! If you're not interested I'll leave it for the security guard."

"No! I'm fully recovered from the tamales and a bit

of fish sounds spot-on. I'll be waiting at the door of the Laredo Suite to tip the porter. And, Casey, thank you for such a thoughtful gesture. Quite civilized under the circumstances. I'll see you tomorrow."

Civilized? Circumstances?

Did that refer to her feelings about his profession? Or something worse? Her curly roots prickled at the thought.

"No thanks required, Barrett. As we say at Hearth and Home, it's my pleasure to serve you."

She picked up the sack of food and headed for the elevators.

"And as they say in Texas, you ain't seen nothin' yet, pardner!"

In his custom-made pajamas and favorite leather slippers Barrett made a groggy shuffle into the sitting room and retrieved a bottle of water from the fridge. As he drank deeply his eye caught the flash of color from the grinning fishes stuck to his hand.

Casey Hardy.

Was this interesting woman simply being kind or was she up to something? Caring for his cuts was one thing, but delivering dinner was another entirely. While the former act had been spontaneous, the latter was deliberate and required at least some planning. Within fifteen minutes of introduction, the lady had made her feelings about his mission quite clear. She didn't like it. And she had given signals that she didn't much like him, either. So what was driving her late-night concern for his nutritional needs?

A light tap, tap, tap signaled the arrival of the bell-man. As Barrett pulled the door open he caught an enchanting scent, not at all the fish he was expecting. And the reason for that stood before him, beguiling eyes gleaming as a small smile twisted her lips.

"Good evening, Barrett." Her gaze swept his buttoned-up appearance. He self-consciously stepped behind the door so that only his head was visible.

"Forgive me, I'm not dressed for company," he explained.

She waved away his concern, clearly amused by his modesty.

"It's my fault for showing up at this unearthly hour." She held a brown sack aloft. "But I think you'll be glad I did."

A mouthwatering aroma wafted across the short distance.

Mmm… English fish and chips! He imagined it… deep-fried, crispy batter drizzled with tart malt vinegar, dipped in creamy tartar sauce. The enticing thought made his spirit ache for the home eight thousand kilometers away. His stomach grumbled for food.

"Now that I think of it, I am a bit peckish. Why don't you let yourself into the sitting room and I'll be right out?"

He left the door standing open and slipped into the bedroom. When he returned with the hotel's signature pink robe belted securely, she was sitting at the small table. The large paper sack had been torn open at the seams and flattened as if a table topper to protect the polished surface.

The woman was thoughtful. Something he'd become unaccustomed to.

As he settled into a chair with the table separating them, she filled two paper plates and chatted as though her appearance at his door was most natural.

"Thanks for letting me come up and share my dinner with you."

"It's not as if you gave me a choice."

She cast her eyes downward in a look of contrition he didn't buy for a moment.

"Would you have turned me down if I'd called to ask?"

"Probably…" He smiled when her head popped up at the answer she clearly was not expecting. "…not," he finished.

Satisfied with the caveat, she continued.

"Late-night comfort food is meant to be shared. It's a Hardy family tradition. Actually, it's more of a weakness. Anyway, my condo is on the other side of the causeway, too far for Captain Jack's to deliver. But the Galvez is smack in the middle of their zone, so here I am." She halved a still-steaming filet and dragged it through the puddle of ketchup on her plate.

She closed her eyes to appreciate the taste, giving him the perfect opportunity to admire her smooth complexion and dancing curls. Where he'd ended the day as limp and wrinkled as an empty sausage casing, she was every bit as appealing as she'd been during their meeting in her office hours before. Then he recalled her attire at their introduction and realized this vision of perfection before him was only one perspective on Miss Hardy.

How many more were there?

"Ah, so this isn't concern for my well-being, after all," he observed.

Her gaze met his. He popped a vinegar-soaked chunk of cod in his mouth and waited.

"Sure it is. Partly," she admitted, and then busied herself arranging a pile of chips. "I could have gone the other way and picked up fried chicken but eating alone is no fun. For either of us. And as long as you're here anyway, I thought you could tell me all about London. I may have business to conduct there soon and I could use some expert guidance."

"You're asking a barrister for *free* advice?"

He couldn't hold back the smile. She responded with innocent, wide eyes.

"Not entirely free. I paid for lunch *and* dinner, didn't I?"

"True. Very true. And all selections have been enjoyable, so I suppose I do owe you. Why don't you e-mail your questions to me and I will answer in a day or two when I have some quiet time."

"Quiet time?" She cocked one brow. "Between me

and the Cowboy Cartel you're gonna experience America Texas-style for a few days and there's nothing quiet about that. With luck you can have quiet when you're back home this time next week." She nodded and popped a fat chip into her mouth. The set of her chin said she expected no further argument.

So, she intends to have me under surveillance until she can get me out of town, does she?

Keeping her enemies close seemed to be more than a Zen Post-it for Casey. Well, two could embrace that philosophy.

And it didn't hurt that this woman was the prettiest assignment he'd had for a long time.

Chapter Four

At 4:00 a.m. the lobby of the hotel was hushed. Only the squeaking of Barrett's rubber soles against the granite floor broke the silence.

"Good morning, sir." The concierge spoke softly. "May I offer you some coffee?"

"Thank you, no. I consumed an entire pot in my suite hours ago."

"Trouble sleeping?"

"Actually, I slept quite comfortably even considering the amount of fried food I ingested yesterday. My body clock is still adjusting to the time difference so I've been wide-awake and working for hours."

"There you are, Westbrook!" a male voice boomed. Doc Moseley stood in the hotel's grand entrance, sporting a Cowboy Cartel cap, his boots planted wide as he waved Barrett over.

"Let's get a move on before the wind kicks up any

more. The marina's gassin' up the *Albemarle* right
now and the bay's gonna be rougher than a cob pretty
soon."

"Are you sure you wouldn't prefer to reschedule?"

"Mercy, no! As long as the good Lord provides a
new sunrise I'll always pick the worst weather for
fishin' over the best weather for workin'!"

Barrett stepped into the predawn darkness and
basked in the ocean breeze that whipped his hair.
Although fishing would never be his first choice, he
had to agree with Doc's assessment. The majesty of
the open sea had never failed to produce an intimate
connection with the Heavenly Father. Childhood
holidays at the seaside with teeth chattering and a
body prickled with gooseflesh were the fondest of all
his memories.

Just as he reached the cab of the enormous red
truck with the interlocking "C" logo on the door, the
darkened window slid down to reveal the passengers
in the backseat.

"Good morning, Counselor," Casey chirped, more
cheerfully than she felt.

Barrett's dark brows drew together a bit. The rest
of his face remained impassive, seemingly not surprised to see her.

"Ah, so it is."

"Casey, scoot over toward George to make room for
our boy here," Doc instructed before climbing into the

cab and slamming the door, giving them no choice aside from compliance.

Manny twisted from his position behind the wheel. "G'mornin', son," he offered.

George followed suit with a similar greeting and handed Barrett the custom headgear they all wore. "It's nice to have you young folks join us."

"The pleasure is mine, sir," Barrett answered as he took the cap and tugged it on. "It was kind of you to include me."

"Yes, thanks for letting me tag along, too," Casey added.

"Little lady, you know you're always welcome to join us. But I gotta admit you coulda knocked me off my feet with a dried cow chip when you asked us to swing by for you." Manny leveled his gaze, telegraphing that he knew she was up to something. "I'm glad you finally decided to take a day off. I don't reckon you've missed a morning roundup with the crew in the ten weeks since we broke ground."

"Well, Cooper's always telling me to let go of his six-shooter 'cause he knows what he's doing. I figured this was as good a time as any."

Manny nodded in agreement then eased the big Ford dually across Sea Wall Boulevard to begin the five-minute trip to the Galveston Yacht Club, where the Cartel kept a state-of-the-art tournament boat at the ready.

"Casey, it sounds as if you put in long days," Barrett observed.

"My family says if I billed by the hour *like some professions—*" she gave the Brit to her right a poke with her elbow "—I'd be able to buy a bank in Grand Cayman. But it's less about the money and more about repaying my family's faith in me by always giving a fair day's work."

"That's an understatement," George chimed in. "This woman can and does work circles around our best crew six days a week."

"And during siesta break she pitches horseshoes with the boys. Some of 'em can't speak a word of English but there's no language barrier once they get into that pit," Doc contributed with a chuckle.

"You'll turn my pretty little head with that flattery," Casey teased.

"No, it's true!" George insisted, leaning forward to see Barrett in the dimly lit backseat. "Then her winnings go to buy everybody pastries from that little Mexican bakery across the street. At two bits a ringer, you gotta be a natural to pocket that many quarters every day."

"Impressive," Barrett agreed.

She'd enjoyed the local notoriety for mastering the Texas-style sport so quickly. Even old-timers like Cooper said she had the touch. But winning was simply like breathing, something she did without thinking.

"Oh, you guys make too much of a little meaningless competition." She gave a dismissive swipe of her hand.

"Meaningless?" George let his jaw sag to his chest to exaggerate his point. "If it got any more heated out there we'd have to nozzle up the fire hose to cool down the game. Pablo is never gonna get over you challengin' his undisputed position as pit champion."

"And I'll earn the title permanently before this project is finished."

"Well, at the rate we're movin' you'll wrap your store in record time. And I must say on behalf of the Double C that we'd never have known this was your first project from the ground up."

Casey felt Barrett's weight shift on the seat beside her as he tensed. She pretended to check the lace on her Top-Sider to steal a glace at the man to her right. His forehead furrowed above arched brows, just as her father's did over the expectation of an upcoming checkmate when they squared off over chess. So, the discovery that she was a novice at this work made him think she was somehow trapped, huh? Well, three very wealthy men within arm's length would disagree. Could she carefully coax a reference out of them?

"Thank you, George."

He returned her smile, a gleam of white teeth peaked through a salt-and-pepper goatee.

"That kind of compliment is what makes the sleepless nights preparing for my quality certification worth the investment. By the way, how's that advice I gave you working out?"

"You know what?" He slapped a palm against his

thigh. "Once we took a different look at the problem like you suggested, I realized we were goin' about the solution all wrong. Like a hound dog with a head cold, we were barkin' up the wrong tree."

Manny spoke up. "But ya wouldn't pay heed to me when I tried to tall ya the same thing."

"Oh hush, you old buzzard!" Doc thumped the back of his hand against the arm Manny rested on the pickup's console. "Given the same choice, who would *you* listen to? A grizzly old cuss who graduated high school number ten in his class of twelve or a pretty filly…"

He twisted to look her in the eye. "No offense meant, Miss Casey."

"None taken," she assured him with an encouraging wink.

"Or a pretty filly with more degrees and awards than Carter has little white pills?" Dock looked to both of his partners for agreement.

"No contest," they chorused.

It was all she could do not to puff on her nails and buff them against her chest. She never personally relayed any of her credentials, but just as Cooper had predicted, the Cartel had done their homework and learned it on their own.

Thank You, Lord.

Barrett's exhale was barely loud enough for her to hear and she felt him relax against the seat back. Was the shift in his body language relief over her credibility or acceptance of their equality?

Either way, he got the point. Hopefully.

Manny lowered the driver's window at the guard gate as a craggy old fellow shuffled out of the security booth.

"Howdy, Nolan. What's the fishin' report got to allow?"

A face weathered from too much sun poked inside. Squinty eyes peered through thick glasses as he identified the newcomers.

"Mornin', Mr. Fernandeeeez, sir." Nolan drawled out the name, then nodded respectfully to the rest. "Bad day. The Gulf Stream's so warm the reds are schoolin' on the bottom, too lazy to feed. Goin' out would be a waste of time unless you're in the market to get your lid blowed off."

"Well, don't that make you wanna spit!" Manny snatched his cap free and tossed it on the dash. "I guess we can burn the fuel to try to prove you wrong, but you've never steered me off course yet."

"Thank you, sir." Nolan blinked. "You folks still need me to check you in? Cook's got cheese grits and belly-burner sausages on the menu today."

Manny turned toward his backseat passengers. "Can we at least buy you breakfast, Westbrook? Sorry about gettin' you out of bed for nothin'."

"On the contrary, few things appeal to me more than sunrise over open water. Would it be possible to purchase a temporary pass at your club? I'd like to procure a double-handler for the morning if rentals are available."

"In this wind?" Casey demanded in what the family called her outside voice. Definitely too loud for the truck.

"The wind is what it's all about." His response was calm, as if reassuring a child.

Doc nodded his agreement. "But you don't need to purchase diddley squat. Any part of this place we didn't build ourselves, we funded with membership fees that are higher than a cat's back. We won't hear of you paying for anything. Just wouldn't be neighborly."

"You heard the man, Nolan. Call ahead and tell them we're dropping a guest of the Cartel off at the marina office," Manny instructed.

Barrett looked from one man to the next; all heads bobbed in agreement. Then his gaze rested on Casey's as if asking for a unanimous decision.

"I think you're crazy, but it looks like a done deal to me," she agreed. "We can leave you here and send someone back later this morning, or whatever you'd prefer."

"I'd prefer you remain here and accompany me."

It was neither question nor invitation. He waited for her response while the tip of his tongue made a quick pass over his lips.

If not for the accent, she'd have sworn her brother had issued the statement. It was just the right blend of assumption and dare. His face remained impassive but humor sparked his eyes. He seemed to enjoy this unexpected turn. Had he seized the opportunity to repay her surprises with one of his own?

Her palms grew moist, pinpricks surged through her fingers.

"Great idea, Miss Casey. My Becky Beth says the ocean spray is better for keeping your skin smooth than anything Estée Lauder ever put in a bottle. And it'd do you good to spend a day away from the site."

"Breathe some sea air," Doc chimed in.

"That's probably true." She did her best to ignore the sudden racing of her heart. "But I honestly don't have the time—"

"Oh, I see," Barrett interrupted. "You made an exception for a fishing trip but you can't carve out a few hours to show a visitor some kindness?"

She felt sweat break out at the roots of her hair. The assumption-slash-dare was obviously intended to get her goat. There was a hungry cat gleam about his pupils. Apropos, since she felt like a fat mouse in the corner, too slow to make it to the safety she was beginning to realize she needed desperately to find. Normally, she'd like nothing better than to best a man at his favorite pastime but she recognized the symptoms bearing down on her.

Not now, God!

She tried to remain calm, to make her deep intakes of breath seem casual.

"Here we are," Manny announced as they pulled to a stop beneath the portico.

Barrett swung the door wide and stepped down. Before he could push it closed, Casey slid across the bench seat and hopped out behind him.

"Think I'll run inside to see that Barrett has everything he needs," she announced.

"Do you mind if we come back for you later, Casey?" Doc checked his wristwatch. "I wanna catch the early-bird newscast. Those environmental purists are on the warpath again. Need to see what they're up to."

"Sure, go ahead. I'll call for a ride." Casey tapped the cell phone clipped to her waistband. "Sorry to rush off, but I need a comfort break," she explained as she stepped around Barrett and made a beeline for the entry.

She pulled the heavy door wide and fought the urge to sprint toward the ladies' room. Once inside a private cubicle, she grasped her T-shirt and swept it over her head, flinging it along with her cap to the floor. She pressed her back to the cool stainless-steel wall and gulped air, unable to get enough oxygen. A paper sack would prevent hyperventilation but she hadn't carried one in her handbag for ten years.

Casey trapped her hands between her thighs in an effort to control the trembling. Sweat trickled beneath her arms and down her sides as she hung her head, squeezed her eyes shut and waited for the misery to pass. After some of the longest minutes of her life, the surging of her heart seemed to level off. She collapsed on the closed toilet lid, propped her elbows on her knees, dropped her head and prayed.

Chapter Five

Barrett faced a wall-mounted bulletin board and studied the listing of sailboat rentals as he waited for Casey to join him. The woman was sticking to him like warm currant jam. He pressed his lips together to suppress a satisfied smile. Everything her wily old foreman had said about her was true. What had he called her? A cap pistol? A strange term but now that she'd popped off a couple of times the comparison was understandable and oddly appealing.

There were physical attributes that appealed, as well. The thick ringlets begged to be untangled, the flashing blue eyes were lethal and her lips appeared dangerously kissable.

Get a grip, Westbrook. This is business and your future is at stake. Handle this with care and keep your baser instincts in check.

Caroline's deceptive acts had befuddled him. He'd

been an idiot to take her at face value. And for his trouble he'd been made to look a fool when the woman he'd believed in, even if not loved, had betrayed his trust.

Now, he had reason to suspect this Casey. Her erratic behavior was certainly an indication she was up to something. Expressing her distaste for his profession over lunch, then hours later availing herself of his company for dinner and outings. It was unlikely she was simply being a good hostess. In fact, all signs indicated she was keeping an eye on him. In any case, he'd return the *courtesies* if she ever showed back up.

Whatever did women find so intriguing in the lavatory?

"Sorry to make such an abrupt exit." Her voice was soft, almost weak, but grew louder as she approached from behind.

"No regrets are necessary. Have you sailed before?" he questioned casually, not making visual contact as they stood facing the wall. A six-meter cutter had caught his attention. The same model his youngest brother Colby raced, Barrett was experienced with the small craft. The water truly was a bit rough this morning, but a brief dunk in this warm gulf would be soothing compared to the race when he'd capsized off the coast of Edinburgh in the frigid North Atlantic. When she made no response, he turned his attention away from the rentals.

Her entire countenance had changed. The color had

left her cheeks. A fine perspiration shimmered above her upper lip. Her mouth had become a flat line, the flesh around it pale in the artificial light. The bill from her cap cast a dark shield over her eyes.

"Casey, are you feeling poorly? We're not even on the dock and you already appear seasick." Maybe teasing her into agreement hadn't been such a good idea. The last thing he wanted in his boat was a nauseous female.

"I'm fine."

He stooped to peer beneath her orange cap, to see her eyes. Small lines of anxiety radiated from the outside corners. She squinted as if blinded by the soft, incandescent lighting.

"You seem in pain," he assessed, feeling a stab of guilt for contributing to a woman's discomfort. Exactly why he'd been an abysmal failure at prosecution.

"Just nerves. It happens occasionally. Maybe if you tie me to the mast I'll feel secure."

He tipped his face to the ceiling to enjoy the laughter that rang out in the quiet room.

"You find that amusing?"

"On many levels. I doubt you realize it but being *tied to the mast* is a term used in settlement contracts."

She shook her head slowly, miserably, her face downcast. "I meant like the story of Ulysses."

He put a knuckle beneath her chin and gently raised her face so their eyes met.

"Yes, I know. But *Calypso* was many times over the size of the boat we'll be on today. The mast on the cutter is only about this big." He made a circle with his thumb and middle finger. "It would be no match for your weight even though you're a skinny little thing."

Her eyes brightened a tad.

"You think I'm a *skinny little thing?*"

"Absolutely."

"Thanks." Her mouth relaxed, color began to seep back into her lips. "I haven't been called that since I was a kid."

"Well, you're not much more than a kid today."

She opened her mouth as if preparing to protest. Her illness seemed to be passing quickly.

He held up a palm. "At least compared to me. I'll be forty in September. Ancient." He stooped over, pretended to hobble with a cane.

It was her time to laugh, though with half a heart. "If fifty is the new thirty as they say, that makes you a college student."

He straightened. "If only that were true."

"You enjoyed that time of your life?"

"Ah, it was the best," he admitted. "And I dragged it out as long as possible. If it wouldn't have been shameful to let Stanton and Colby enter the practice before me, I'd still be at university."

"Stanton and Colby? Your brothers?"

An ornamental ship's bell chimed the hour.

"See here, miss. You're stalling to distract me, aren't you?"

She hung her head, nodded.

"Would it be such a horrid thing to go out on the water with me this morning?" Something made him hope that was not the case.

"Could we just wait a day or two till the waves settle down?"

"Frightened of the water, then? Sink like a rock, do you?"

"Not at all. In fact I'm a strong swimmer. But sailing's an area where I have zero experience and I prefer some advance notice and prep time for a new activity."

"Ah, a control freak, as Americans say."

"My family calls me the Warden. I run a tight prison."

Hmm, a new piece of the puzzle fell into place. He'd dropped in unannounced on a lady executive who insisted on calling all the shots and did so from first light to lights out. If he didn't give her back some of her own control, he might never get his job done.

"Very well then, Warden. What do you fancy at five-thirty in the morning that won't require too much warning or preparation?"

"A strong cup of coffee."

"Done."

Her mouth curved into a smile and her eyes filled with…gratitude.

Where the front office had been quiet, the dining room was lit with activity. Fishermen who'd chosen a cozy breakfast over a beating at the hands of the elements sipped from thick white mugs and ate from matching platters laden with beefsteaks and eggs.

Barrett studied the daily specials. The odd choices were paper-clipped to the plastic-coated menu that doubled as a place mat.

"What's a belly burner?"

"It's a sausage link so hot you can count on indigestion."

"Done." He slapped his menu on the wooden surface, nodded agreeably toward the server and held his empty mug aloft. She winked at the universal signal for coffee and carried a pot to their table.

Dressed from head to toe in shocking-pink, her name tag identified their waitress as Tavia. She nodded approval at Casey's simple order of oatmeal with raisins, then looked to Barrett.

"I didn't notice soft-boiled eggs on the menu," he mentioned.

"That's because cook only knows one way to boil an egg and that's hard enough to bounce it off the wall. How about fried, over easy?"

"Sounds perfect. I'll have a double order of your belly burners along with fried tomato, baked beans and two eggs prepared as you recommended."

Tavia scribbled on her pad, cocked a painted-on eyebrow and muttered, "It's your heart attack."

She turned away with a smart crack of her chewing gum.

"So, tell me about your brothers." Casey ripped open two yellow packets and dumped the sweetener into her cup.

"Ladies first. Give me the story on these nerves of yours."

She brought shoulders to her ears in a shrug. "It's not a big deal. I have a lot on my mind and I guess the heebie-jeebies got the best of me."

"Were you *heebie-jeeby* just now?"

"And part of last night," she admitted.

"And how do you deal with this?"

"Distraction is the best medicine, so I work till I drop."

"Don't tell me the warnings I've heard about powerful female Yanks are accurate," he teased.

"If you've heard we're smart, hardworking and goal-oriented, then the stories are absolutely on target." A gust of wind buffeted the glass windows beside their table. Her jaw tensed. "So how about a rain check on that sail?"

Her question was hesitant, just shy of a plea.

"If you prefer," he agreed, deferring to a woman's wishes as his mum had taught. "I shall honor your request. Does forty-eight hours' notice work for you?"

"I'll make it work."

"Then our first negotiation is settled."

He leaned his elbows on the oak tabletop and graced her with a smile that almost made her forget the claustrophobia she'd experienced fifteen minutes earlier in the ladies' room. She hadn't had an attack in years, had been certain the disabling episodes were gone forever. Taking to her bed to sleep it off was out of the question with this guy up in her business. She'd just have to focus on one breath at a time and make small talk.

"I appreciate it." She thanked God for Barrett's acquiescence. She couldn't board the *QEII* right now, much less a jon boat with a broomstick for a mast.

She felt her shoulders relax and some of the tension ease from her spine. If she could make time for a full-body massage that might help, but there weren't hours enough in the day to get her work done, much less get pampered. And here she sat wasting time over breakfast, albeit with a perilously gorgeous man who could make or break her future.

"So, tell me about this family who likens a fetching young woman to a corrections official." He sipped black coffee, his eyes glinting like gunmetal above the rim of his cup.

"Brutal, huh?" Casey still remembered the vacation when Guy had labeled her the Warden. Even she had to admit her seven-year-old determination to tell everybody where to bunk for the week had earned her the stern moniker.

Barrett nodded, his forehead wrinkled with sympathy. For the first time she saw the resemblance Savannah had mentioned the day before. And while Casey had no particular attraction to the bad-boy actor, at this particular moment she simply wished Barrett was anybody other than who he was. There was something about him she wanted to like. To trust. And on another day in another time she'd happily have climbed into a life raft with him in high seas without warning!

What are you thinking, Rebecca Thelma Casey Hardy? As hot as he is, the man is still from the same school as those opportunist vultures who brought the case against H & H. They're all in it for the money and Barrett has made it clear a couple of times already that the financial bottom line is at the bottom of his concern. Shake it off and do whatever it takes to protect the family and still accomplish your goals. And straighten him out on that "female Yank" comment while you're at it!

"I agree, Casey."

"Huh?"

"That it's a brutal nickname. Warden, I mean."

"Actually, it's somewhat flattering no matter the original intent. I take that as a bit of a compliment as the youngest of six kids with thirty-six uncles and aunts and one hundred and twelve cousins."

"Oh, my!" His jaw dropped, exaggerating his shock. He pressed fingertips to his chin and closed his mouth. "Sorry." He grinned in the most charming way.

"It's okay. That's the usual response, so we're used to it. Big families like ours are kinda rare these days."

The waitress arrived and served their orders.

"Are all those relatives invested in Hearth and Home?"

The question was so casual she almost blurted out a response. Instead she drizzled honey into her bowl and swirled it with her spoon. Was he poking into her personal finances or just making friendly conversation? The latter was unlikely, given the purpose of his visit.

She could almost hear her father's soothing voice. *Just shoot straight, kiddo.* So she did.

"At first they were all heavily invested, but once we were in a position to go public, most decreased their holdings. But everyone still supports us, of course." She nibbled at her oatmeal while he chewed a second link with gusto and no apparent reaction to the sausage laden with cracked red pepper.

He wiped his fingers on a paper napkin and took a long swallow of ice water. She'd only had belly burners once since arriving in Texas and that experience had required antacids for a full twenty-four hours afterward.

"How about you, Barrett? You're part of a family business, too."

"Well, I'm trying to be part of it anyway."

"Trying. That's an interesting way to put it."

She scraped the burned corner from a triangle of toast and buttered it lightly, wondering if what he'd just said could be used to her advantage.

"Our firm has been serving clients for nine generations and we've divisions that cover every conceivable facet of the law. Unfortunately, I've tried them all and none suits me. The study of the craft is more to my liking than the practice of it."

"You're still a young man. It's not too late to follow your heart and go the academic route."

"My family lives by the adage 'Those that can, do. Those that can't, teach.'"

"So your parents don't approve?"

"Approve?" He scrunched his forehead. "They don't even know."

"That's incredible. With me it's always been just the opposite. I put my parents and siblings on notice ten years ago that I'd be CEO of H & H one day. My father is sixty-seven and with my only brother settling down in Austin it looks like I'll get my shot at the position before I'm thirty-five."

"What about your sisters?"

She waved away the absurd thought as if batting at a pesky fly.

"They're as much into their kids as I am my career."

"Could all that ambition be the reason for your heebie…"

"Jeebies." She licked a drop of honey off the back of her spoon and shook her head. "That goes way back before it ever occurred to me to run a corporation that would generate billions in revenue."

Barrett nodded and dug into his eggs.

"So, power and control appeal to you."

"It's not about appeal. It's about achieving the goals I set for myself during college, and seeing the fulfillment of my strategy for the company. I can't be happy with anything less."

"Well, then. It seems you're just the sort of executive my client hopes to engage."

And once again he gave her a smile that would charm any starstruck female. Her stomach clenched and sent a shockwave of shivers throughout her system. Was it the thought of making headway on her plan or the appeal of the man seated across from her? They were interchangeable now, and she was beginning to wonder which one she truly found most exciting.

Chapter Six

Later that day, Barrett parked in the shade behind the construction office. He made a pass around the American luxury sedan, admiring the sheer size of the automobile as he pulled items from the trunk.

Though it was well after the lunch hour, there was only one vehicle out front and no activity at all across the way at the site. Maybe the crew made allowances for the humidity and took breaks out of the reach of the simmering rays. An appealing thought as he moved into the heat.

When he turned the corner and started up the steps to the landing, he was pleased that no one was around to hear his stomach give a menacing rumble. He'd been a fool to eat even one of the evil breakfast sausages, and a glutton for eating four. A glutton for punishment, that is, and punishment was exactly what he got an hour after consumption. Too much delicious but strange food had his insides in turmoil. It was fortunate Casey hadn't wanted to sail or he might have embarrassed himself by losing his meal over the bow. A brief nap and a cool shower had put him to rights and now he was ready to pore over the documents she'd agreed to make available.

Savannah must have heard his approach.

"Good afternoon, Barrett." She stood in the doorway and extended her hand. He shook it carefully, admired her gentle touch and wondered if the spunky brunette was Casey's friend or strictly a professional understudy.

"The same to you, my dear. Where is everyone?"

"They're dealing with a situation on the far side of the building, but I told the boss lady I'd stay here and take care of you." She motioned and he followed her inside the cool structure.

"I've set a pitcher of tea on the conference table and there are several folders Casey said you'd need. Please make yourself comfortable and yell if I can get you anything else."

He took a long swallow of the icy drink. The sweetness that had seemed syrupy at first try was amazingly refreshing and tasty. He was further amazed that Casey, a suspicious woman he'd met only yesterday, had overcome her mistrust and left a barrister in her workplace without supervision. He spread the folders before him, took out a legal pad and began to explore the details of Hearth and Home's expansion plan.

Halfway into his first page of notes, the door to the outer office sprang open with a thump to the wall behind him. Barrett heard heavy boots stomp across the threshold and then Cooper's voice.

"This kind of stuff makes me want to give up my chew and go back to smokin'! Of all the bad luck Miss Casey could have, this takes first prize."

Barrett pushed his chair back and quickly strode to the reception area.

"What's happened to Casey? Has she fallen jeebie again?"

"Jeebie?" Cooper asked, his face a wrinkled mask of confusion and surprise. He obviously hadn't expected to encounter Barrett.

"Where'd you hear that term?" Savannah moved closer, her lips puckered in concern.

"For a brief time this morning she wasn't feeling well and that's how she described her malaise."

He noted the way Savannah nodded slightly, and seemed to file the detail away before she changed the subject.

"Casey's okay. But there's been a bit of a find on the property."

"A bit of a find?" Cooper's voice rose, indicating the comment was an understatement. "A twenty in the hip pocket of your jeans is a bit of a find. Karankawan artifacts in your construction zone is a blasted nightmare. Those tree huggers will be crawlin' on this place like ticks on a huntin' dog."

"Would you mind explaining, sir?"

Cooper spit tobacco juice into the ever-present dis-
posable cup and jangled his keys. "Casey won't like
it, but there's nothin' gonna stop you from findin' out,
so you might as well go on over there and see for
yourself." Cooper stepped out on the porch.

"Let me lock up and I'll come with y'all." Savannah
pulled her ponytail through a baseball cap, put enormous sunglasses on her nose and yanked the door
closed behind them, turning the key in the lock.

"Coop, let's take your Wrangler so we can go
straight across." The young woman squeezed between
the two seats and settled on the back bench. "You ride
shotgun, Barrett."

"Shotgun?"

"Just take the front seat, buckle up and hang on,"
Cooper instructed gruffly, obviously in no mood to
explain the firearms reference. He backed up abruptly,
threw the vehicle into Drive and then went careening
toward the area under construction. As they rounded
the frame of the partially drywalled building, he
stomped the brake. Thick white dust swirled around
them, clinging to the dark slacks Barrett would likely
burn after this Texas adventure had ended.

A small crowd could be seen. Some knelt while
others stood and leaned in for a better look at whatever
held their interest in the center of the circle. The
vehicle had stopped only meters from the group, yet
no one turned to identify the newcomers.

"We're lucky the press ain't here yet."

Just then, as if on cue, a van with a cable station logo pulled alongside the Jeep, sending even more dust flying. A reporter with his microphone at the ready motioned for the cameraman to begin filming and stay close. He caught up with Cooper as he climbed to the ground, so obvious in his H & H shirt.

"Parker Pearson, Eye Witness News. Is it true? Could this really be the biggest Karankawan find of the century?"

"Settle down, dubs. The century's young and it's just some pots and piles of oyster shells. It ain't like we uncovered a Mayan pyramid."

"Still, there hasn't been a local discovery in years. This is big news. Has the historical society been notified?"

"Not officially, but I'm sure you'll take care of that."

"Stand over there, Chuck. Shoot me from the left."

"Just call it your good side and get it over with, Parker." The man known as Chuck rolled his eyes and hoisted the camera to his shoulder. "It's not like we don't know about that big mole on your right cheek."

"Noonday news with Parker Pearson here. We're at the site where a new Hearth and Home supercenter is under construction and set to open in less than ninety days. We've received a tip that Karankawan artifacts were unearthed here only hours ago and the cache of pottery and utensils may be the most notable in decades. Excuse me." He elbowed his way through the building crew and pressed forward toward Casey. "Ma'am, are you the member of the Hardy family who's managing this construction?" He spoke to her but smiled for the camera lens.

Not dressed much differently than she had been when they'd parted ways at 7:00 a.m., Casey tilted her head back and peeked from underneath the signature orange cap. In her hands she cradled a beautifully preserved liter-size clay bowl with fish painted end to end around the lip. She held the earthenware aloft, gently brushing away the years of dirt.

"Look, isn't it magnificent? I've never held anything like it." Her eyes, which Barrett found much more magnificent than the dusty old basin, sought his. He smiled to reassure her, though it didn't appear she felt the worry Cooper had expressed.

"Miss Hardy!" Pearson grasped for the artifact as if to save it from destruction. She pulled it protectively to her chest as he continued. "That piece could be over four hundred years old. You must be careful."

Several cars had come to a stop nearby and a dozen newcomers rushed the site.

"We declare this location sacred Karankawa territory!" one shouted.

"Don't touch another thing!" the next insisted. "You could be unearthing a burial ground. Who knows what kind of spirits we could be disturbing."

The band of local activists moved into place before the camera.

"Oh, for pity's sake." Cooper stepped forward and inserted himself between the small frenzy and Casey. "This stuff gets turned up all the time. I've lived in this neck of the woods for sixty-six years and everywhere you dig a hole from Galveston to Corpus Christi you're likely to unearth spearheads and hunks of pottery. There's nothing sacred or spiritual about it."

"That's for the authorities to decide," the newsman chimed in, facing the camera again. "This is Parker Pearson for Eye Witness News at the site that will become Galveston's only Hearth and Home supercenter. Or will it?"

He snapped off the wireless microphone.

"What's that supposed to mean?" Casey stood, still cradling the antiquity. Her eyes lit, pools of bright indignation.

She focused on the anchor she recognized from the evening newscast, trying to make sense of his comment.

"It means beware the CAVE people."

"Cave people?"

"Citizens Against Virtually Everything. Once they show up in force, they're going to shut you down indefinitely."

The recent arrivals began waving their crudely made signs and chanting. "Protect our native heritage! Stop the expansion!"

"What are they talking about?" Casey looked to

Peterson for an answer. "They don't have a single detail and they're already carrying on like a bunch of flower children at a sixties' protest."

"Interfering with commercial growth on the island is the life work of this bunch. You should see the frenzy they can get whipped into anytime the port authority tries to expand services." He turned his back and motioned for his cameraman. "Come on, Chuck. Let's go shoot that tanker that's leaking oil in West Bay."

"But what happens now?" she called.

He glanced over his shoulder and gave her the grave look he'd used for the camera. "Hire yourself a good lawyer and settle in for a fight. Unless you find a way to reason with these kooks, they can hold up your construction for months, maybe get your building permits revoked and shut you down permanently."

"Permanently!" She stared at the pottery in her hands and then up into the dark eyes of Barrett Westbrook, the ninth generation of British attorneys. His face was impassive, unreadable. Was that because he'd just had all his questions answered? Would he call for her conviction and execution before evidence was even presented?

Her fingers started to tingle. In anticipation of the trembling that sometimes followed that sensation, she turned the handmade vessel over to Cooper.

"Don't worry, Casey girl." He put a warm hand on her shoulder. "I've watched these folks for years. They may seem goofy but their hearts really are in the right place. We need a few days to figure out how big this campsite was and then we'll take it from there. The Karankawas were nomads, so maybe this is one of those spots where they only stayed for a little bit before movin' on."

"Then how would you explain this perfect jug? Why would something like this get left behind? It doesn't make any sense. What if this is only the tip of some cultural iceberg?"

Cooper held up his other hand to silence her growing alarm, and leaned closer for privacy.

"There are plenty of authorities on this stuff. Let me make some calls to see what we can find out."

She felt her pulse quicken. Turning something of this critical nature over to another person went completely against her grain. Tingling shot through her toes, her hands trembled noticeably, and the mask of her face buzzed. If she didn't get away soon she was likely to faint in front of everybody. Wouldn't that be a sight for the cameras!

"Trust me, Casey." Cooper gave her a side squeeze, just like her daddy would have done. "Your brother hired me for this purpose, now let go of my six-shooters."

A small smile returned to her face. Guy trusted Cooper. She would, too.

"Okay, I'll head over to the office to give Dad a heads-up on this development."

"Don't be upset if he wants your brother to come

down from Austin. It's only a few hours' drive and it might be a good idea to have him here."

Over my dead body.

She'd reassure the family she had it under control and then she'd go the condo and stick her head under the covers for a few hours. In college sleep had been a peaceful escape, but that had been so many years ago. Why was this plaguing her now, of all times?

"Come on, kiddo. Let's get you over to the trailer so you can take care of business." Savannah snaked her arm through Casey's, held tight and tugged toward the Jeep.

"It's okay. I've got you," she whispered. Her best friend had noticed. Of course she would. She'd been the one to get Casey through these episodes back in college. At a time when she'd thought she was losing her mind, Savannah had been the one to point out that there were only two states of being for the Hardy family… *In control and out of control.* Each family member handled it in their own way, but at the end of the day if calling the shots wasn't an option, there were consequences. For Casey, it had been this anxious feeling she'd labeled the heebie-jeebies. It was horrible to have the body she'd conditioned so well through sports and competition betray her in this way.

Just thinking about the bothersome symptoms made her stomach churn. During a full attack, hot needle pricks would shoot through her hands and feet until they trembled and went numb. Her heart would pound, her body would break into a clammy sweat and vertigo would knock her off her feet. As the surge subsided she'd be weak and nauseous, fearful it would return. Knowing it could strike without warning and with a vengeance.

There was no room in her life for such distraction, such fear. The store was on track to open in record time. If she could stay the course, she'd beat all of Guy's previous records and still secure the partnership of Barrett's client.

Barrett.

Casey's gaze swept the quickly gathering crowd in search of the Brit who was reassuring, handsome and charming in equal parts. And at the moment he was…

Gone.

Chapter Seven

Barrett moved casually among the locals. The group continued to increase in size as word of the find spread. Several had cell phones pressed to their heads, acting as the island's town criers. Their excited chatter grew as each leaned over the haphazard excavation site to catch a glimpse of the crude contents.

"Will you look at that, Clayton?" one woman declared, tugging the checkered shirttail of her companion. "Nobody's laid eyes on it for hundreds of years. Don't you feel special?"

Odd what Americans considered old. They'd be positively enthralled with the well in the courtyard of his London townhome. Romans had dug and lined the well with stone a thousand years before. Now *that* was a hole in the ground worth peering into.

Clayton responded loud enough for everybody to

hear. "Stoppin' these rich out-of-towners from chewing up another hunk of Texas history is what makes me feel special. Why, companies like this'd bulldoze and pave over the Alamo if they thought they could make a buck. And if we don't stand up and protect our heritage then our forefathers fought the American Revolution for nothin'."

Barrett bit the inside of his lip. Not to keep from speaking, but to keep from smiling. These people didn't sound much different than he himself had only a few days earlier during his snobbish tirade with Sig. Hadn't he used much the same twisted logic when he'd tried to convince his father that a stint in the States wouldn't produce anything but confirmation that the Wild West was still wild? Had his father also stifled a grin knowing Barrett would encounter a little prejudice of his own?

Lord, thank you for giving me that smart old chap for my dad! Barrett offered up in gratitude.

And now what was he to do with this new personal as well as professional insight? He could dispose of this mission quickly by returning to the construction office and combing the available files for further damaging details. Then he could have a quiet dinner as he wrote a report that would justly condemn moving forward with this deal.

Imagining the disappointment in Casey's eyes brought tightness to his chest. He brushed the dust from his trousers and the image from his mind.

As interesting as he found the lady and the Lone Star State, England and duty beckoned him home.

Business was business.

And this business was his last chance.

The construction office was silent when Barrett let himself inside. Carpet cushioned his leather soles as he returned to the conference area to retrieve his attaché case. He glanced toward Casey's open door as he stepped past and saw the beauty seated behind the desk with her slender hands clasped tightly atop her blotter. She'd freed her thick hair from the cap and rested her head against the back of the tall leather chair. With eyes closed, she whispered the Savior's name over and over, more a plea than a prayer.

What a stark contrast to the picture of control and efficiency she'd projected when they'd first met.

Could that have been only yesterday? He'd spent months with Caroline yet he'd never seen as many sides of her as he had in one day with Casey.

Was it because Caroline lacked such depth? Possibly. A twinge of guilt shot through him at the judgment. In fairness, he'd done little to encourage her to reveal herself beyond social facets where she most definitely glittered.

Was it because the woman before him, undoubtedly in distress, was willing to expose her weaknesses? Unlikely. He was probably the last person on earth she wanted or expected to observe her at this moment. He backed away, prepared to turn from her door, when her eyes fluttered open.

"Barrett."

She said his name in a disturbing manner, as if it were associated with finality. That's how he made her feel, as if all were lost? So, this is what the latest effort with Westbrook Partners would reveal; that he was the Grim Reaper. And if he went to the hotel and continued with the plan, was that what he'd be?

The killer of dreams?

Casey's dreams?

"Sorry, I didn't think anyone was here," he apologized. "I'll get my files and be on my way so you can deal with this unexpected turn of events."

"There's no rush." She sounded tired, defeated.

"Dad says this isn't the first time we've had to interrupt construction because of environmental issues, so it's not quite as bad as it seems."

Was she making light of this grave concern for his benefit or her own? With a woman determined to call the shots and with so much at stake it was difficult to discern the difference.

"What will you do now?" As he said it he realized he truly cared about her answer.

He cared about this complicated young lady.

"We'll let the crew take some time off with pay while we investigate. Those guys have been working hard, sometimes seven days a week, so they deserve it."

"And I'd lay odds you've also been on the job nonstop so this is an opportunity for you to get some rest as well."

"My work *is* my rest."

"With all due respect, it seems as though work is your distraction from rest…Warden." He added the last with a smile, hoping she'd understand he meant it kindly.

Her hands relaxed. She lifted one and pressed it to her heart.

"Point well made," she agreed. "Aimless downtime scares me but I seem to thrive on orderly chaos."

"Then come with me. I have just the pandemonium you need to take your mind off this new development. I promise that afterward you will rest like a newborn babe."

Unconcerned for the work that needed to be done or for the soreness and wounds from his tumble on the rocks of Tintagel, he stepped around the desk and held out his hand. She made no effort to take it and pressed closer to her chair. His heart withered a bit. He was not exactly a man about town, but neither was he accustomed to ladies shrinking from his touch.

"Oh, come now." He thrust his hand closer. "It won't be as unpleasant as all that."

With reluctance she slipped her palm into his and he gently tugged her to her feet.

"I'm not dressed for anything fancy." She stated the obvious as she glanced down at her work boots and jeans.

He reached for her cap, spun it backward and

tugged it over her head. Sable curls poked through the plastic fastener.

She was adorable. Her inviting lips only inches away.

He blinked several times to erase the disturbing thought. He really needed to wrap up business and get off this island, and out of this state known for extremes before he did something extremely inappropriate!

"Well, then. Let's be off." He bowed slightly, swept his hand for her to go before him.

Casey paused at the exit to allow Barrett to get the door for her. So, this new-world all-American girl had some old-world expectations. An enchanting discovery.

He twisted the knob and as she passed he couldn't resist tugging a lock and watching it bob back into place.

It was the same gesture Guy always used; stretching a curl to the fullest extent to see it recoil like a spring. But Barrett's teasing touch had a much different feel than anything her brother had ever inflicted. Taking such a liberty seemed out of character for the stuffy man who'd appeared without warning a day ago. The offer of his hand had been a caring gesture and now he'd touched her hair, and not in a brotherly way.

At least she hoped not. Moments earlier the compassion in his eyes had made her chest ache. Maybe

Guy was right. Barrett Westbrook didn't seem anything like the opportunistic attorneys who'd helped bring the personal injury case against Hearth and Home. If anything, this man appeared to be just the opposite.

She settled into his car. While he placed his brief-case in the trunk she sent up a prayer.

Father, instinct tells me Barrett can be trusted. Have You sent me someone who might understand what I'm going through? If this situation is not Your will, please close my mouth. I desperately need to talk to somebody besides Savannah.

He slid into his seat.

"Right, then. Let's be off."

"Where to?" she asked as he tugged his seat belt tight and slipped on an expensive-looking pair of dark glasses.

"Must you have all details in advance, Nosy Rosey? Can't allow a chap the element of surprise, eh?"

"Sorry." She pulled out cheap shades and adjusted them on her nose. "The surprise we just got was enough for one day, but if you say I can I'll trust you."

"Dare I hope this means you've changed your mind regarding the legal profession?" He flipped the air-conditioner on high as they merged with midday traffic.

"American women are permitted to do that, you know."

"My dear Casey, female prerogative is not limited

to this country. If men are fortunate, they learn that valuable lesson early on. I credit my own dear mum's guidance with saving my brothers and me untold misery and confusion on that subject."

"Tell me your brothers' names again?"

"Stanton and Colby. They're both younger and far wiser it would seem since they've been cultivating their fields of expertise for years and I've yet to even identify mine."

"I still think you should consider teaching."

"Too many generations of Westbrooks have served at the bar. For me to lecture on the law rather than practice it would be tantamount to treason." He sifted thick dark hair through his fingers and shook his head. "My family could not accept it and I would never ask them to."

She nodded, understanding his point but from the opposite perspective. Here was an intelligent, extremely well-educated man who should be at the height of his career and instead he was still fluctuating on his specialization. By contrast, she'd known exactly what job she'd wanted for as long as she could remember having professional aspirations. By the time she was old enough to pay attention, Hearth and Home was already a market competitor. The family dream had made the bricks and mortar her reality.

And her own dreams began so early in life that she couldn't recall a time when she didn't intend to be at the helm one day. She hoped against hope that driving force was not at the root of the unnerving episodes that struck for the first time when she was a college freshman.

"Isn't it interesting that we come from very different backgrounds, yet our basic values are the same?" she noted.

He eased to an intersection light, pushed his shades up on his head and gave her his attention. "How so?"

"Neither of us can bear the thought of family disapproval."

"Ah, so we can't. You suspect we're neurotic?"

"I'm positive I am. Savannah called me on it years ago. Give her another day or two and she'll diagnosis you, as well." Casey grinned and he returned her smile. For the first time since he'd appeared, she relaxed. A gut check told her she had to ease up. She had no choice if she wanted the early-morning heebie-jeebies to be an isolated occurrence.

Barrett left the Strand and turned north on Holiday. Casey realized he was taking her back to the marina. The stiff wind that had accompanied sunrise had died down but the water was still choppy. Would he try to get her to sail again? She felt her nails dig into her palms.

"Don't get your nerves in a twist. We're only going for a stroll."

She curved her mouth, knowing the smile and the behavior were lame.

He'd spotted her fisted hands. Was that because he cared or was it just another sign of his training? And what did it matter? He'd recognized her discomfort and tried to set her at ease. It was enough.

"Thank you." It was her turn to reach out to him. She laid a palm gently on his forearm where he'd rolled up the sleeves of his dress shirt. He took his left hand from the wheel and patted her fingers lightly. Reassuringly.

"My pleasure." He didn't withdraw from the touch.

For Casey, the moment that followed was as unsettling as it was comforting. His skin was warm where her fingers rested on his arm and the soft pressure of his hand on hers was so pleasant. Her heart thumped hard. She felt it in her temples, certain it had to show. There was a special something about Barrett. Something she wanted so much to believe in. A quality she'd never experienced. She was thirty years old and for the first time in her life she felt a…felt a…*connection.*

Had she really only met this man? What would it be like to know him for a lifetime?

Now where on earth had *that* thought come from?

He returned both hands to the wheel, swung the big sedan into the visitor's parking area, made a wide arch and screeched to a stop astraddle two spaces.

She braced her feet against the floorboard.

"Quite an entrance, Dale Ernhart Junior."

"Thank you. I've never operated a vehicle this large and it's going well, don't you think?"

Was he serious?

"Absolutely," she fibbed, just in case.

"But I'm actually the fourth."

"Huh?"

"Barrett Wesby Westbrook the Fourth."

She sucked her lips against her teeth to hold back a smile. It was a wasted effort as a grin broke free.

"I know, it's dreadful, isn't it?" he admitted.

"Almost as bad as Rebecca Thelma Casey Hardy."

"Great gobs of mushy peas!"

The mock horror on his face punctuated the silly expression. He would be a hit with her nieces and nephews.

"That name *is* a mouthful," he agreed.

"Tell me about it."

"Shall we?" He swept his hand toward the board-walk.

She nodded agreement and waited while he rounded the front bumper to open her door. When he popped the trunk, and signaled that he needed a moment, she leaned against the fender and lifted her hair to expose her neck to the hot sunshine.

"I always travel with a pair of trainers, and I brought them today just in case," he explained while he exchanged his leather dress shoes for sneakers.

"Just in case a Native American encampment shut down my job site?" She was still in shock over the discovery.

"No, but as long as that's the case we may as well take advantage of the afternoon break."

"What about your work?"

"I can do that in the hotel tonight. That is *if* a certain young lady will go home and get some rest and allow me to be productive."

She looked around, pretending to search for this person he mentioned.

"Yes, you." He finished tying his shoelace and slammed the trunk shut. "Unless, of course, your plan is to keep me so busy I can't accomplish enough to make an educated recommendation."

Her breath caught in her throat. Was it so obvious?

"Uh-huh, so that is your strategy. Clever girl."

Evidently so.

"Can't pull the wool over your eyes, can I, Counselor?" she recovered as best she could.

She turned toward the boardwalk, not yet sure where to head other than away from his piercing glance. He fell into step beside her. "And so far the plan's not working out too well," she admitted. "I try to stick by your side every minute to make sure you don't find anything negative to report, and bad stuff is all you come into contact with."

"Other than my body's response to tamales and belly burners I'd say all observations have been quite interesting, even if not entirely positive."

"Yeah, I'm quite interested myself to see what Cooper finds out about those artifacts."

"Did you contact your corporate attorney?"

"Dad's taking care of that. If we can't resolve this locally in a day or two, they'll send representation."

"It appears you have the right persons working the situation. So try to give this burden to them and trust our Lord to work it out for the best."

She stopped short, tipping her head back to see into his face. His eyes were covered, giving no clue to his earnestness. But neither were there lines of emotion in his face to indicate he was poking fun or testing her.

"You're a believer?"

"All my life. Raised in the Church of England from the time I was a lad, but only came to know Christ personally during my early years at Oxford. I actually considered the seminary for a brief time."

"You're not serious."

"Indeed I am. As I said earlier, not staying the family course has never been an option."

"So you decided against it?"

"Only after a good deal of prayer. I came to realize the secular world was in desperate need of a Christian legal advocate."

"So, the family convinced you to continue with your law degree?"

"Actually, I never discussed it with anyone other than our parish minister. This is the first time I've spoken about it since."

"Wow, that's quite a revelation. I'm honored you'd share it with me."

"You seem trustworthy enough. I don't think you'll give away my secret."

"Are you making all this up so I'll drop my guard?"

He stopped walking, reached into his pants pocket and pulled something out for her inspection. A smooth silver disk the size of a nickel glinted in the sunlight. He turned the piece over as he placed it in her palm. The simple outline of a fish was etched into the metal.

"Take it, it's yours."

"Oh, Barrett, I couldn't."

"I insist. It's a physical symbol that we agree to trust one another."

As she opened her mouth to object, the wind whipped her H & H hat from her head and sent it tumbling end over end down the dock, into the water's edge.

"I'd say He concurs." Barrett pointed skyward. Then he sprinted to the spot where the orange glow was drifting beneath the surface. He used a nearby dip net to retrieve the sodden cap, then positioned it atop a piling.

"Thank you, Sir Lancelot."

"My pleasure, Lady Guinevere." He bent from the waist, took her fingers gently and brushed the back of her hand with his lips.

She giggled like a silly girl but the alternative was to shiver like a love-starved old maid. She pulled her hand free and stuffed it into her hip pocket.

"While we wait on my cap to drip-dry, where's this pandemonium you mentioned?"

He watched her withdraw an elastic band from behind her back, capture her hair and expertly fold it close to her head in a thick braid. Even so, fat corkscrews sprang free and danced about her face.

"Come with me."

She fell into step beside him, the soles of their shoes thumping the wooden planks that lined the perimeter of the marina. High overhead the sun beamed hot, glinting off surface ripples that slapped against pilings. Uprights were secured with old tires serving as bumpers between the dock and the hundreds of watercraft that would navigate the bay during the summer. Everything from wakeboarders to luxury yachts floated in the slips.

Awnings on tall posts shielded some craft from the heat and blocked their view of the activity across the cove. They rounded the dock and he watched with interest for Casey's reaction. As he'd hoped, her mouth popped open, a silent "Oh" on her lips. She removed hot-pink shades and squinted into the distance, confirming that the vessel before them was real and not an illusion. Flying a flag of thick white, blue and red stripes was a three-masted tall ship. Her crew swarmed the deck in a frenzy of activity as they checked and replaced hundreds of meters of rigging.

"Oh, my! I didn't know this ship was here!"

"I saw her posted on the notice board this morning. She's Russian, owned by the St. Petersburg Marine

Science College. The engineering school uses her for sail training."

"And I see why." Casey drifted forward as if in a trance, drawn to the carefully orchestrated activity on the masts high above the deck.

Barrett smiled at her face alight with interest and joy. She would likely take to the sight of sailing vessels in Plymouth like an English lad to Christmas pudding.

"What's she called?"

"The *Mir.* It's Russian for *peace.*"

"Ah, like the space station." Casey never looked away. Her gaze was transfixed on the ship before them.

"Exactly."

"I'd love to go aboard a craft like that one day."

"Then we shall." And as he said it he knew in his heart of hearts that somehow the casual statement would become a reality.

He waited for her reaction but none came. Had she heard him? Was she not even curious why he'd said such a thing?

"They work so fast and with so little communication, like they're on auto pilot," Casey praised the sailors.

"As they should. Climbing thirty meters above the deck to haul and set sails, you'd best be confident in your team. Life literally depends on it at sea."

She turned to face him, admiration evident in eyes the same azure-blue as the water behind her. Finally he'd managed to get her attention.

"How come you know so much about this stuff?"

"The English are a sea-faring lot. I suppose we're naturally predisposed to be curious about it. But for my brothers and me sailing and racing have been almost obsessive since we were in short trousers."

"In that case, the next time you invite me out on the water with you I will accept without reservation."

"Then how about a sunset cruise this evening?"

Chapter Eight

A pile of castaway clothes lay rejected on the bed. He'd said *dress for dinner* and nothing even remotely suitable remained in Casey's closet. She glanced at the clock on the night table. Three hours. Barrett would pick her up in three hours and all she'd settled on so far was shoes. And while Jimmy Choo peek-a-boo pumps made a lovely statement, they wouldn't have quite the desired impact if she coupled them with a World Cup commemorative T-shirt and threadbare camo pants.

Savannah leaned against the door facing her, arms folded in disapproval of the options. She surveyed the mess with a sad shake of her head.

"Girl, I've been telling you for weeks that the few men you don't scare off with the Warden's uniform you run off with the steel-toed boots and hard hat."

"I can't help it if that's all I own."

"Yes, Casey, you can. You make an obscene amount of money and there are stores that will gladly take it from you and give you haute couture in exchange."

"I don't have time to shop."

"You make time to shoe shop."

"That's different." She hugged the pair of five-hundred-dollar silver sling-backs to her chest.

"Well, if you want a second date with this cutie-pie you'll need something appropriate for the first one."

"This is *not* a date," Casey protested. "I'm just making sure he's a happy camper so he'll turn in a positive review."

"If that's entirely true, put on Brooks Brothers and sensible shoes and just focus on the work."

Casey's shoulders slumped. She hadn't had anything even remotely resembling a date in ages. The idea of a dinner cruise with a movie-star-looking hunk of a man made her weak in the knees. But all foolishness aside, this evening really was about business. So much was at stake and everything seemed to have taken a downward turn since Barrett's arrival. There was no denying that from the moment he'd shown up she'd had one problem after another.

The last thing she needed tonight was trouble.

"I'd loan you something of mine but there's not enough meat on that scrawny body of yours to do my clothes justice."

Casey had to agree that she was a stick figure while Savannah was a figure eight.

"Hey, how about that hot little sundress you wore for your brother's wedding rehearsal?"

Casey perked up at the thought, then immediately wilted, realizing the silky scarlet strapless and matching bolero jacket were in the bottom of her closet. Weeks ago she'd tossed the pieces there, too tired to hang them up after dinner with the Cartel and their wives. Wardrobe maintenance had never been her strength, hence the proliferation of navy suits, the target of so much teasing.

"I already wore that dress. It needs to go to the cleaner's."

"Did you get anything on it?"

"No, but it's more wrinkled than a paper napkin after a Happy Meal."

"Where is it?" Savannah slid hangers inside the closet crowded with work attire. Casey stepped around her friend and squatted to retrieve the horribly creased pieces off the carpeted floor.

"See?" She held them for her friend's inspection.

Savannah took the slivers of expensive red fabric and pressed them to her nose for a sniff test.

"Oh, this is nothing a little steam and five minutes in the dryer won't fix. Come with me."

Thirty minutes later the ensemble had been softened by exposure to a steamy shower, tumbled in a warm dryer and pressed to perfection by a hot iron.

"Good as new." Savannah draped the outfit across the bed and smoothed it carefully.

"You're a lifesaver." Casey praised her friend and opened her arms. The two hugged and rocked side to side, celebrating one less obstacle in their lives. "Thank you so much for agreeing to come down here with me." The words caught in Casey's throat. Her four sisters were a part of her, inseparable in their own way. Even so, there was an age difference between Casey and her siblings sufficient to leave her feeling misunderstood from time to time. Finding her dearest friend in fifth grade had been like discovering her other half. They communicated volumes with few words, physically experienced one another's joy and sorrow, and picked up on vibes that even family might miss.

"And where else would I spend the summer after you dangled cowboys under my nose?" Savannah grabbed her oversize shoulder bag and began to search the contents as she commented casually, "You have plenty of time and you really need to catch a catnap."

"I've got it from here, mom." Casey made light of the instruction.

The riffling stopped as Savannah raised eyes filled with compassion. "Honey, Barrett said you had the heebies this morning, and I saw for myself how your hands were shaking. No brave face is necessary with me. If they're back, and my gut says they're not, we'll deal with it just like before. Together."

Casey could only nod, her throat too tight for words.

"I remember they seemed more frequent when you were worn-out. So while I take care of things around here, you go lie down," Savannah insisted, never needing a signal to give a few instructions of her own.

Casey nodded, knowing the comment was accurate. She trusted her friend's instincts and prayed they were on target as usual. She had to be at the top of her game and the game seemed to be changing by the hour.

The woman gliding toward him was a stunning vision in clingy scarlet that revealed sculpted arms and shoulders. Glittery open-toed shoes accented a red pedicure as she strode beneath the darkened portico into the late-afternoon light. Barrett's lungs expanded as he sucked in a fast breath.

"Wow," he whispered. He stood ramrod-straight beside the Cadillac, then whisked off dark shades for a better view.

Casey in jeans and work boots was adorable. All-business Casey dressed in her power suit struck an authoritative pose. But this very feminine creature in evening wear, carrying a tiny jacket, was spectacular. Casey in red was a sight to behold. His palms itched to slide up sun-kissed arms and rest on her shapely shoulders.

"Good evening, Barrett."

As she moved within arm's length he took her hand and twirled her in classic ballroom fashion for a slow look at all sides of this vision.

"Good evening, my beauty." His voice quivered with an odd yearning quality he hoped she couldn't identify. He leaned from the waist to place a soft kiss on the back of her fingers as before, allowing his eyes to feast again.

His chest ached. He wanted desperately to fold her in his arms.

"Breathtaking," he added simply.

Her eyelids fluttered, and she ducked her chin as if unaccustomed to compliments. The action was exquisitely genuine, neither coy nor calculated.

"Thank you." Her response was brief as she allowed him to assist her into the big sedan.

"Thank heavens I brought a jacket. I should have worn a tie, as well." He was woefully underdressed to accompany her. "I trust I won't embarrass you."

Her eyes grew wide.

"Was I wrong to assume dinner is somewhat formal?"

"Well, her majesty won't be making an appearance this evening, but the brochure said it would be a memorable occasion. Maybe we'll be the couple who makes it so."

Couple. Saying the word felt right.

But how could that be? Why was he having these intense thoughts after such a brief time when he'd never had them in months of a previous relationship?

He put the vehicle into gear and reminded himself of the purpose for this visit to Galveston.

Visit?

That sounded so cheery. When had he started thinking of it as anything other than an imposition? He shook his head at the absurd change in his attitude. He needed to redouble efforts in line with his goals and stop this romantic nonsense regarding the woman beside him. There was work to do for the firm, credibility to build with the family, a unique niche to carve out where he would be valued and respected. This was no time for personal foolishness.

"If you've changed your mind, it's okay."

His head snapped to the right. "Beg pardon?"

"You have a scowl on your face and you haven't said a word since we left my place. If you'd rather not spend the evening with me, I won't be offended."

The worry in her soft voice said otherwise. The heart he'd just determined to harden softened even more. By her own admission she'd had a sleepless night. In the predawn hours he'd witnessed a nervous episode of some sort. Then he'd seen firsthand the shutdown of construction and the unwanted attention of the media. He'd taken her back to the marina for a breather and suggested dinner to distract her from her worries, and here he was making her feel badly.

His mum would be very disappointed in her eldest son. Caroline would say it was typical.

He had to make it up to Casey. Atone for his rudeness.

"Sorry. Just concentrating on keeping to the right

of the motorway." He reached across the leather seat to touch her arm, to physically reassure her. And himself. Tomorrow would be soon enough for business.

"It really is all right. I know you're bound to be feeling the effects of jet lag by now."

"Nonsense. The second wind has filled my sails and I fancy sunset on the water with a charming dinner companion."

The corners of her mouth lifted in a small smile.

"Thank you for such kind words, Barrett. I'll try to live up to your expectations."

"Casey, I have no expectations," he insisted. "Let's just have a nice evening, shall we?"

"I'd like that."

She turned her face away, presumably to enjoy the array of pleasure crafts in the bayou as they crossed the 61st Street bridge.

The self-confidence she possessed in spades at some moments was elusive in others. He made a mental note to add this instability to his list of items for consideration.

"Oh, check out the riverboat!" Casey pointed toward the triple-deck paddle wheeler. Her enthusiasm was back, and her skin absolutely radiated as if lit from within. When the woman was feeling good it was impossible not to be swept along in her wake. "I haven't been on one of those tourist traps since I was a kid and our family used to take us sightseeing on the Mississippi."

Barrett reached into the breast pocket of his jacket and withdrew the brochure he'd obtained from the hotel concierge. What had seemed like a good idea hours earlier was suddenly childish.

"The paddleboat tour of Offatts Bayou seemed a nice alternative since it's still a trifle windy for an open-water dinner cruise. I should have thought to ask you first. Would you prefer to dine elsewhere?"

"Goodness, no!" Large round eyes and a big smile told him she was sincere. "I haven't had a chance to experience any of the local attractions since moving to Galveston. My only downtime has been spent flying home to present progress reports to the board. I could see Moody Gardens from the bridge but it was always just a tease because I never had time to get any closer."

"So you don't mind spending the evening as a tourist?"

"Not as long as you're trapped with me."

"I can't think of a nicer place to be." And he meant it from the depths of his soul.

The private dining area on the top deck was well appointed for very special occasions. However, the fresh flowers, white linen service, attentive staff and sumptuous meal were secondary to his extraordinary companion. After two hours of being regaled by stories of the Hardy clan, Barrett was certain his destiny was somehow tied to this place. This woman. The question was whether that certainty was good or bad. It could be either in equal measure.

He put a huge spoonful of sweet potato pie into his mouth.

"Heavenly choice," he mumbled over the spicy dessert served with a generous dollop of heavy cream.

"I figured you could have cheesecake back home."

"Very true. All your choices were spot-on." He hardly knew how to pronounce things called *jamba-laya* and *étouffée,* let alone whether they would appeal to his palate. So, he'd asked her to make the selections once they'd been presented with menus.

She waited while the waiter presented their after-dinner coffee. When they were once again alone she pulled out the chair next to her and began to shift his cup and saucer to the unoccupied place at her side. Since it seemed she expected him to change seats, he made the move without question. As soon as he was settled the reason for her actions was obvious.

"Ahhhhhhh…" he breathed.

"I thought you'd want to see that."

A spectacular sunset was about to take place. An orange glow blazed on the horizon with fingers of fire shooting into the deep blue of the darkening sky.

"To me, the only vision more incredible is daybreak," she shared. "I believe the message of the sunrise is the promise of a new beginning with new mercy."

"Mind if I take a note?" He withdrew a pen and

copied her words on a cocktail napkin while she looked on.

"You flatter me, sir."

"I'm pleased that's the by-product, though it's not my intent. I couldn't help noticing the snippets you've posted in your office. I, too, love to capture the unique turn of a phrase. Most of my notes come from the least expected places and uncommon speakers, though I have plenty of Shakespeare and Churchill in my journals."

"So you've actually created books for yourself?"

"Over the years."

"I'm not nearly so organized. I jot interesting phrases on Post-its and display them on mirrors and whiteboards. Then if I relocate, I stick them in the pages of a spiral notebook. When I get to the new place, I slap the ones that pertain to my situation on the wall for wisdom and encouragement."

"Contemplation and meditation. Your moments of Zen."

"You remembered." The quality of her voice, the awe in her words, was a reward.

"I wrote it down."

"So I've joined the ranks of great poets and world leaders?"

"In my book, yes." He wanted to add that she also topped his short list of amazing ladies, blessed with beauty and ability. But it was too soon to pay such compliments. Wasn't it?

She opened her small handbag, fished out a folded newspaper clipping and smoothed it before him on the table.

"Here's something funny for your book." The glint in her eyes told him he was in for a laugh at his own expense.

He read the cartoon out loud. "'And God said, "Let there be Satan, so people don't blame everything on me. And let there be lawyers, so people don't blame everything on Satan."' Quite amusing."

"I thought so when I clipped it out of the paper this morning."

"Well, just to show you I can take a joke, here's one for you. What do you call a smiling, courteous person at a Bar Association convention?"

She shrugged and waited on the punch line.

"The caterer," he deadpanned.

"Good one." She laughed at his silly one-liner.

With humor sparkling in her eyes she was even more appealing. What wouldn't a man do to win her heart?

"Barrett, not everyone hates lawyers."

"That's only because not everyone's met us." He couldn't resist the obvious opportunity to make her laugh again.

"Ouch! Now remember you said that and not me." She wiped at the corners of her eyes where merriment gleamed after a fit of giggles.

She sobered and pointed to the space between the sea and the sun.

"Oh, Barrett, look! How incredible."

The gap closed steadily as the ball of light drifted closer to the ocean's surface. The steam engine powering the huge wheel of paddles quieted as guests moved to the starboard to fully appreciate the view. As the blaze of yellow-orange kissed the sea and quickly sank into the deep, three bells sounded followed by the applause of the guests.

Thousands of tiny white lights sprang to life, twinkling like countless stars overhead. Live music drifted up from the deck beneath them and the two soon found themselves in privacy as diners went below to enjoy the unusual jazz.

"What is that?" He tapped his fingers on the tabletop.

"Zydeco. It's Louisiana folk music in keeping with the Cajun theme this evening. You picked a good night to get a taste of New Orleans. Literally!"

"And it seems I picked the perfect companion, since you seem to know all about these things."

"Galveston celebrates Mardi Gras just like they do in New Orleans. I was lucky to be here during the season and got a firsthand introduction." She trailed her fingers through colored beads pooled on the tabletop.

"And I was expecting Texas to be full of cowboys and Indians."

Her hand stilled. How he wished he could recall the comment. "Well, we certainly unearthed plenty of that for you today, didn't we?"

She closed her eyes and leaned her forehead against the heel of her hand as if the memory of the day's events had rushed painfully back into her mind. He had to do something to distract her from her worries. To atone.

Anything.

He shifted closer, placed his arm protectively around her and cupped her bare shoulder with his palm. She leaned into him, rested her head and nestled comfortably into the circle of his arm. A long sigh escaped from deep within her: a whoosh of pent-up emotion. Then a soft involuntary sniff punctuated the sigh, as if tears threatened. What to do?

Without asking permission or giving himself time to second-guess, Barrett cradled Casey back enough to tip her face up to his. Her eyes were tightly closed, and moisture glistened where her dark lashes pressed together. He dipped his head, pressed his mouth close to her ear and whispered, "Just trust. The Father will work all things out for the best."

The words were a welcome breath of warm comfort on Casey's ear. The events of the past two days had drained what was normally a limitless supply of energy. Now fatigue had her fighting back tears and in the arms of a man who was not much more than a stranger. A stranger who could be the key to her dreams or keep them locked up indefinitely.

This is crazy, she told herself. *I have to shake this*

*off and get back to business. Too much is at stake to
let this man get so close.*

And then what was innocent became intimate as he
pressed his lips to hers.

Chapter Nine

The kiss was so unexpected, and so incredibly enjoyable, that it had to be imagined. Fatigue had finally overtaken her. She was hallucinating!

The firm pressure of a mouth upon hers and the soft moan that was most decidedly male convinced her otherwise. She cracked one eye ever so slightly then squeezed it shut. Sure enough, she was lip-locked with the gorgeous Brit!

Along with her pulse, her mind raced at a frantic pace. She knew she should end the intimate contact, stop the madness, withdraw from the embrace. Instead she leaned into him, twined both arms around Barrett's neck and pulled herself closer. It had been so long since she'd been kissed, and *never* like this.

"Ahem."

Somewhere, someone cleared their throat. She was too well occupied to be concerned.

"Excuse me, miss? Sir? Will you be joining the rest of your party in the lounge?"

Party? Lounge? The silly questions had to be directed at another couple. They didn't know anybody else on the paddleboat and right now all she knew was how wonderful it felt to be wrapped in strong arms, to feel a heartbeat next to her own.

Barrett raised his head, ending the kiss. Casey's eyes fluttered open to stare directly into his. Sitting so close, his breath was warm on her face, and she could make out silver flecks in his eyes like sparks dancing above a fire. It was hypnotic and she was transfixed.

"Thank you, but no," Barrett responded. "We'd prefer to remain above deck if that's acceptable."

"Certainly, sir. But we'll be discontinuing service up here for the remainder of the evening."

"Very well."

In the silence that followed the waiter's departure, they remained in the embrace, lips only inches apart, eyes staring.

"I must say, of all the things I expected to experience on this journey, this was never a consideration," he admitted. A wry grin curved his oh-so-inviting lips.

"I'm a bit surprised myself. Whatever made you do that?"

"I've always been a fool for a woman in genuine emotional distress. A female reduced to tears on the witness stand would compel me to request a recess.

My trials were interminable, so much so that that none of the partners wanted to sit at the bench with me."

She relaxed her arms and shifted to put some space between them.

"So, that was a pity kiss?"

He pulled her close, held her firmly.

"Absolutely not. I've wanted to do that since the moment I first saw you."

"Even covered with dust and safety gear?"

"Especially so. And I wanted to kiss you again when I saw you in your business suit. And again this morning in your boating attire and again tonight when you walked out in that incredibly appealing dress. Your presence has been an assault on my senses and I confess that maintaining a professional distance has made these two days a constant struggle. And just now when you let worry overtake you, I couldn't help myself. A kiss seemed the perfect diversion."

She pushed out her bottom lip, mimicked the exaggerated pout that always worked for her nieces.

"I'm still feeling worried. I need more distraction."

He took the shameless hint. A smile curved his lips as he lowered his mouth to capture hers. His kiss was slow and soft, neither pressuring nor apologizing. She breathed in his scent, snuggled into his embrace. Returned his ardor.

Then reality struck. He was a man who could cause a great setback to her career plans if he chose to do so.

And she had almost forgotten that.

Almost. She *had* to catch up on her sleep. Rejuvenate.

She ended the kiss, reluctantly slid her arms free and busied herself with her bolero. He stood to help her into the small jacket. Her flesh prickled where he trailed warm fingertips against her bare skin. The breeze whipped her hair.

"You're cool. Shall we go inside to enjoy the musicians?" he offered.

"I'd rather stay up here where it's quiet."

"Then allow me, please."

He swept the suit coat from the back of his chair and draped it over her shoulders. It settled comfortably around her just as his arms had only moments before. This was a man she could be at ease with if only there wasn't the constant threat of his mission.

She inhaled the light fragrance that clung to the fabric. Barrett's cologne. Subtle but so very masculine. She wanted nothing more at that moment than to move her chair closer, to draw warmth from his body rather than his jacket.

Instead she resumed a respectable distance, determined to focus on the professional relationship and make the most of the short time she had to impress him. As a competent executive, *not* a needy female. She'd refuse to think about how absolutely right it had felt in his arms. How utterly perfectly his lips had matched hers.

Details she'd hold close after he was long gone.

She released a sigh at the thought.

He immediately began to apologize. "My boorish behavior has offended you. I was wrong to take such a liberty."

The man noticed everything! She had to get her emotions off her sleeve. She'd start by making light of her concerns, at least so far as he could tell.

"Oh, no." She shook her head. "I cooperated fully, so I'm every bit as culpable. Let's just blame it on the moon." She raised her eyes to the golden crescent that floated overhead.

Barrett would love to charge his feelings to the inconstant moon, but he knew better. What was taking shape inside him was nothing short of incredible. The hiccups his heart knew each time Casey came into view were like nothing he'd ever experienced. He was not a man given to irrational behavior or thoughts. In fact, just about everybody he knew accused him of being too cautious and calculated for his own good. But the very reason he *should* be an excellent barrister seemed to hold him back instead. Was this woman the key to unlocking what he'd waited almost forty years to feel? Emotional spontaneity.

"Let's talk a bit about your personal aspirations," he said, deliberately changing the subject to something safe. Focusing on what she wanted was far safer than dwelling on his own desires.

"Work is my first love."

His stomach fluttered at her mention of the word. But it was love of profession, not of the heart.

"So no husband and children for you?"

"Oh, one day maybe. But I have a huge family, so I don't feel the ticking clock that worries so many women my age. No, I haven't driven myself so hard for half my life to cook dinners and change diapers. I'm not sure that'll ever be in the cards for me."

Again, he felt a deep stab but it wasn't pain so much as disappointment. Why? Because the woman beside him was committed to her career? Wasn't that a good thing in a partner? A *business* partner, anyway.

"How about you? Is your single status by design?"

She stirred a packet of sweetener into her black coffee while she waited for his response.

"Me? Well, I haven't arrived at this ripe old age as an unmarried man intentionally. Stanton and Colby both wed right out of college to women they knew only briefly. That sort of thing quite frankly doesn't appeal to me."

"Define *that sort of thing.*"

"A whirlwind marriage. I believe in courtship. A long period of getting to know a person."

"Ah, an old-fashioned guy."

"Possibly, but more importantly I want to be certain deep down inside that it's right. That it's God's will, a braided cord that can survive any test." He pressed his fist to his heart to make his point. Had he ever said these words to Caroline? No, because he'd never felt it with her, nor with any other woman. So why was he sitting here with someone he'd known for two days putting down the idea of love at first sight when there was little else that could explain how he felt toward Casey?

Love? Egads!

Where was his cautious and calculated nature when he needed it most? He must have left it behind when he'd boarded the flight at Gatwick because it certainly hadn't accompanied him to Texas.

The cool wind kicked up tendrils, whipping in a frenzy about her face. Casey snuggled deeper into his jacket. She reached across the small space between them and placed her left hand on his arm.

"I think that's wonderful, Barrett. I hope I'm blessed with a man who feels the same. My parents come from Iowa farming country and they grew up within miles from each other. They've been married for fifty-three years and they credit that to the bond they share with one another and with Christ."

"Do you think there's room for global travel at this time in their lives?"

Her expression changed ever so slightly. Her brows tipped together and a little of the sparkle left her blue, blue eyes.

"I don't honestly know. They'd never agree to be apart and Mama's Parkinson's makes travel difficult."

She seemed to consider it for the first time. Had she actually thought through all the implications of what she was proposing with his client in London?

"Casey, you do understand there will be meetings in other regions requiring attendance by your chief officer, correct? No alternative representation will be agreeable in some circumstances."

"Well, yes, but I just assumed…" Her speech faltered as she processed the realization. "I assumed other executives, myself included, would be able to manage those demands."

"In some cases, that may be. But my client deals heavily in areas of the world where the culture won't accept a stand-in."

He watched a moment of consternation play upon her face, clouding the eyes that had been alight with enthusiasm moments earlier. Once again he felt guilt for putting the concern there, but if the lady wanted to compete on a global scale she would have to get educated. Quickly.

Could she handle it? The events of the past two days told him she needed a coach, one savvy in legal as well as financial matters. Could she find such a resource in time to make a difference? Either way, that was her business. He'd already crossed enough lines of propriety. The very reason he'd come all this way was being jeopardized. It was time to take a step back.

"I believe it would be to your benefit to acquire a corporate coach."

Her back straightened at the suggestion, as if he'd insulted her.

"I can make some calls and get some recommendations for you," he rushed on, hoping to recover.

"I beg your pardon, but I have an MBA and a black belt in Six Sigma. I don't need mentoring."

"And I have an Oxford law degree as well as acceptance to the Bar Counsel. Even so, I'm a lousy trial barrister who's still looking for his fit in the profession."

"So, you're saying I'm lousy at what I'm doing and I need help finding my fit."

Women!

He closed his eyes and sent up a prayer that when he opened them again Casey would have a smile on her face and this would just be a joke between them.

No such luck. There was most decidedly a crease between her brows and a downward curve to those sweet lips.

Lord, give me the words to backtrack from my misstep!

"That is not at all what I intended to convey." He tried for recovery.

He reached for her hand but before he could capture it she snatched it to her lap, suddenly preoccupied with her white linen napkin.

"On the contrary, Barrett, I think that's exactly what you meant."

"Well, maybe in a way, although I certainly wouldn't

state it in such crude terms. Listen, Casey, you're obviously new to this position and from what I've observed, your training ground is basically on-the-job baptism by fire. There's no shame in that but your learning curve is taking place on some very high-stakes territory and you're asking a foreign investor to take a chance on you. If you won't consider a professional coach, how about bringing your brother back into the equation? Have him come down for the duration of the project."

"Absolutely not." The set of her jaw accentuated the clipped words. "Guy is a newlywed and he belongs with his family. I'm qualified to do this and I will, with or without your support." She twisted the napkin between her hands. Was she imagining it was his neck?

"Did I say I wouldn't support you?"

"Well, that's not exactly why you're here now, is it?"

"No, it is not. But my purpose is suddenly as foggy as a Cornwall morning, because I find that I care about you."

She stopped terrorizing the linen square and raised her eyes to his. There was no joy in her gaze, only confusion and question.

"Is that your offer of casual friendship?" she asked.

"Have you noticed anything casual about me thus far?"

"Now that you mention it, no."

"Then why would you think I would expect something as intimate as a kiss to be taken lightly?"

"Because it is to most men."

"I'm not like most men, Casey. As you said, I have old-fashioned expectations and values. I don't give my affections easily. Nor do I admit my failings publicly, but now I've done both with you. Do you understand what I'm saying?" He lowered his voice to say the next softly. "I care."

She took the hand he offered.

"And in a very surprising way, so do I," she confessed.

His heart thumped at double time at her admission.

"Then let's just take this one issue at a time, shall we? I'm not here to judge who you are or interfere with your plans. I'm here to do a job for my company and my client and I cannot neglect my duties regardless of my personal feelings."

"So you're saying you have *personal feelings?*"

"Blast, woman!"

Throwing all caution and propriety aside, Barrett scooped Casey up. She went willingly, eagerly wrapped her arms around his neck, threading her fingers through the back of his hair. He followed her lead. He had no chance to pull her to him before she lowered her face, pressed her lips to his and kissed him with an intensity he'd never before experienced.

Wow!

For long moments they explored with taste and touch, sharing the supremely intimate contact, exchanging light whispers of appreciation and murmurs of pleasure. She brushed the touch of butterfly kisses to his cheeks, eyelids, brow and jaw before capturing his mouth again.

His mind and his senses were filled with Casey. He wanted her in his arms. Forever. He fought the desire to proceed beyond the chaste. He was a man of some years and she was a grown woman but to go further would be wrong. For both of them and for many reasons. If their relationship progressed it would be under God's terms and in His time.

Oh, how Barrett hoped God would be in a hurry!

Casey raised her face and stared down into Barrett's incredible gaze. She'd never dared to dream of sharing a lifetime looking into eyes so filled with passion and longing. Could this be real? Could two people from such different worlds honestly feel anything lasting after such a short time? And yet, other than geography, were their lives actually so different?

Reluctantly she untangled herself from his arms and returned to her seat beside him.

"I apologize."

"If it has anything to do with your incredible kisses, I shall not accept it." The joke could not mask his voice, husky from emotion.

"I probably should, but it wouldn't be sincere. There are no regrets there." She smiled and touched her fingertips to his solid jaw for emphasis. "I apologize for jumping to the conclusion that you were finding fault with me."

"Recognizing growth opportunities and finding fault are vastly different. You have incredible skills, otherwise you wouldn't be in the position you're in today. And you also have unlimited potential that could be developed with assistance. I can do some research if you'd like."

"No, thank you. But I do appreciate it and I'll take it under consideration. Maybe some assistance with international matters would be a smart idea."

"Your decision, my dear."

The uniformed captain who'd greeted them as they'd boarded approached their table.

"Mr. Westbrook?"

"That's correct."

"I'm sorry to interrupt your evening, but this important message came by radio from the reservation office."

He handed over a sealed envelope and stepped away. Barrett gave the note inside a quick glance and handed it to Casey.

"Your man Cooper is trying to reach you. Do you have your cell phone turned on?"

She pulled it from her purse and noted the signal was too low to receive calls. Cooper had to have tracked her down through the concierge at Barrett's hotel.

"It must be urgent or he wouldn't have gone to this

kind of trouble. My phone won't work out here." A dozen thoughts flashed into her mind at once, all of them critical, none of them good.

"If you'll come with me, we can connect you with your party."

"Thank you, I would really appreciate it." She turned to Barrett. "Would you mind?"

"Of course not. I'll wait here."

In the wheelhouse she steeled herself for bad news.

"Cooper, what is it?" she demanded the moment he answered. Fear of a family crisis had her heart in her throat. What else could it be?

"I'm sorry to scare you like this, Miss Casey, but I knew you'd want time to prepare for tomorrow."

"Prepare for what?"

"The city council is meeting at ten o'clock in the morning and we managed to get on the agenda."

"But we haven't even had time for research. Isn't this sudden?"

"Yes, ma'am, it is. But the longer we wait, the bigger head of steam those crazies will build up against us. And the longer we're shut down, the more money we lose. If you still want to open in record time you've gotta jump on this like a chicken on a June bug."

"You're right, of course."

"I'll pick you up at seven so we can meet with the legal team your daddy's sending down from Houston. They'll be speaking for H & H at the hearing."

"We're going to depend on *lawyers* tomorrow?"

"Unless you've got a better plan."

Casey's heartbeat accelerated. The rush of blood to her head pounded in her temples. Needles of heat shot through her fingers and toes as dinner threatened to rise up in her throat. For fear she'd faint, she plopped down in the captain's chair, leaned her head in her hands and cried out from her spirit.

Help me, Father! For the first time in my life I have no plan at all.

Chapter Ten

She was sinking! Unable to touch the bottom far below. Her hands were leaden, useless. She cried out, but no sound pierced the blackness. The tiny point of light above was too distant to illuminate the silent surroundings. She was deep in the well.

Back in the pit of despair.

Casey bolted upright in the darkened room and tossed off the covers that bound her to the bed. Shuddering, she ran a hand through hair tangled and limp with perspiration. A fine layer of dampness covered her torso, and her light nightgown clung to her skin. Snapping on the reading lamp at her bedside, she slung her legs over the edge of the mattress and pressed her feet to the solid comfort of the floor.

"It's back," she admitted out loud.

She'd lapsed into a restless sleep hoping she'd seen the worst this week had to offer. She'd been wrong.

The episodes were back and now the dream was, too. It was identical to her college years and couldn't be ignored. But she'd managed to overcome the symptoms a dozen years ago and she would again. Savannah said all the classic signs of stress were there. Casey wouldn't waste her time in disagreement as she had back then. Instead, she'd focus on the power of prayer.

The strength and reassurance of the Word.

She twisted her hair and secured it with a clip, then exchanged her gown for a fresh robe. She padded quietly through the fully furnished condo, careful not to disturb her roommate. Savannah's presence was always a godsend, but tonight Casey needed God, Himself. She settled in the cozy living room and took her Bible into her lap. The companion study guide lay on the coffee table where she'd placed it shortly after moving in many weeks ago, untouched and without progress because she'd been too busy with her own concerns to spend time alone with God.

Forgive me, Abba Father. I need Your mighty presence. I need to feel the comfort of Your perfect will. Please come and meet with me through Your Word.

She flipped to the book of Proverbs and began to read in the sixteenth chapter.

Commit to the Lord whatever you do and your plans will succeed. The Lord works everything out for His own ends.

She leaned her head back and closed her eyes to contemplate the words of wisdom. Without exception, those who knew her best said she had control issues. She'd long since accepted that the judgment was both accurate and uncomplimentary. She'd only ever sought counsel from Guy on the subject, which had ended in a huge fight when he'd said she wanted to be CEO because she loved calling the shots, making all the decisions and not allowing anybody to give her guidance. When he'd stepped down and recommended her for his position, her brother had warned her against getting too wrapped up in climbing the corporate ladder. But instead of listening to the voice of experience she'd insisted on doing things her own way, hardheaded and proud of it.

Had she ever intentionally committed her work to the Lord? Asked Him to be the author and perfecter of her plans as well as her faith? Her mama said most folks used prayer as the last resort when it should be the first. It seemed Casey had also made that mistake, but it was never too late to correct it.

She slid to her knees and bowed her head before the Lord of all creation.

Father, forgive my stubborn nature. When You send me guidance, please give me eyes to recognize it. Open my mind and make it fertile ground where the seed of new ideas can grow. And when I encounter advice I'd just as soon not hear, I beg You to shut my big mouth. Teach me to use my ears to listen just in case the words are from You. And give me the intelligence to know when to forge ahead and when to cut my losses and leave well enough alone. This is all new territory for me, Lord. Go before me and show me the way. Your way.

I don't know what my plans are now, Lord, but I commit my efforts to You and ask You to work everything out for Your own end. Amen.

With a lighter heart, she rose and curled up on the sofa where she rested her head on the thick cushion and drifted into a dreamless sleep.

"Casey, honey, Cooper's at the door. He says he's here to pick you up."

Savannah, in Tweety Bird pajamas, was perched on the edge of the coffee table. Her hand gripped Casey's wrist, still gently shaking as if uncertain the message was getting through.

"What time is it?" She shot upright and blinked at the light that streamed between the slats in the wooden shades.

"It's a little after seven. I thought you'd be sleeping in but he says you have to meet with some lawyers in a few minutes."

"Oh, no! I didn't hear the alarm!"

She dashed to the bathroom to splash water on her face. The nubby pattern from the sofa cushion embossed her cheek.

"We have an audience with the city council this morning and my dad sent some legal support down from Houston. We're meeting with them to prepare for the hearing."

"Why didn't you fill me in on this last night?"

"It was so late when Barrett dropped me off. You put in just as many hours as I do and I didn't have the heart to wake you."

While Casey brushed her teeth and twisted her hair into a knot, her friend handed over the Warden's uniform as she was ready for each item. The end result lacked the polish that came from taking her time, but stepping into her new pair of lemony yellow Manolo Blahnik's gave her the boost she needed to face the ordeal ahead.

Casey admired her feet in the full-length mirror, enjoying what might be the last secure moment of the day.

"What would women do without designer shoes?"

"Oh, I don't know. Maybe donate all that money to homeless shelters?" Savannah winked to soften the comment.

"Gee, thanks for going easy on me this morning."

"You have the rest of the world for that. You have me for the truth."

"Girl, I need you to be praying today that the truth will set us free. If the city decides to revoke our building permits even temporarily we could be in for a legal fight."

"How can I help?"

"Look after Barrett when he shows up. Let him

take over the conference room for the rest of the day, keep him fed and give him whatever he needs, but keep a close eye on him. The guy's so intuitive he scares me."

"Well, you seem to have won him over, so he should be in your corner, right?"

"Don't make the mistake of thinking that even for a minute. He's here to do a job for his family and their client, not H & H. If he thinks this deal is going south, it's his responsibility to pull the plug on our future."

"Honey, there will be other opportunities," Savannah insisted.

"But there will never be another *first* opportunity. I won't settle for failure." Casey's voice was firm.

"And you don't think you can reason with him?"

Casey couldn't help laughing at the statement.

"The man operates on pure reason. We'd have to appeal to his emotions and I get the distinct impression those are pretty well off-limits." Her chest tightened as she said it, remembering his simple declaration... *I care.*

"Don't confuse his culture with his emotions, Casey. English folks naturally project that whole stiff-upper-lip thing, but underneath they're softies just like the rest of us."

"From your lips to God's ear." Maybe there *was* hope.

She hugged her friend, grabbed her briefcase and dashed for the door.

* * *

The council chamber resembled a courtroom. It gave Casey the creeps to take her place at the speaker's table before the panel of local officials. The morning's briefing had been unnerving. Maybe it was time to consider lawyer-avoidance therapy, if there was such an animal. She knew she was blowing things out of proportion and it was impacting her work relationships, but it was so hard to forgive and forget the painful months she'd watched her family and their reputation suffer.

"As we discussed, Miss Hardy, this will probably go faster if you'll let me do the talking," the man at her right murmured. His voice was annoyingly low and calm.

Based on their business cards, Gerald Hempstead was the senior of the two representatives from the Houston-based law firm and an expert in these matters. She pressed her lips together in an effort to exercise self-restraint and give the control to someone else. What if this was the guidance she'd been praying for in the wee hours of the morning? Didn't she owe it to God to keep her mouth shut, open her ears and render her mind fertile ground for new seed?

"Good morning, ladies and gentlemen, and thank you for attending today's open session of the Galveston City Council." An elderly man in oversize horn-rims greeted the room. "It is always encouraging to have the participation of our citizens."

"These folks aren't *our citizens*," a sarcastic male voice called from several rows back. "All you have to do is check out those Harris County license tags to know they couldn't care less what happens on the island as long as it won't interfere with their sunbathing and Mardi Gras partying."

"Nathan, you'll get your five minutes," the mayor responded without so much as a glance up from her notepad.

Nathan? Not only was the heckler known by name, the mayor didn't appear to be in the least disturbed by his outburst. Casey laced her fingers together in her lap. This couldn't bode well for their side.

Casey peeked over her left shoulder to the aisle just behind them, seeking out Cooper for a comforting sign. His bushy white eyebrows were drawn together, his mouth curved upside down in a line of disapproval. His lips were pressed tight, like he wanted to spit, and for once it was not related to the lump of tobacco that was perpetually tucked inside his jaw. Clearly, Cooper was worried.

"The sergeant at arms may continue," the mayor instructed.

"Thank you." He moved into a list of topics to be covered, finishing with the previous day's discovery. "We have a good news/bad news issue to consider today and Her Honor has graciously agreed to move it to the top of the agenda. Since a recent find of Karankawan artifacts has temporarily stopped the building of Galveston's first Hearth and Home store, we've invited all interested parties to speak."

"I got plenty to say, so how about if I go first?" Nathan's voice called.

The mayor removed her reading glasses, passed her hand over her eyes as if preparing for the worst and then nodded agreement. "After we've had a brief review of the issue, you may be the first to respond." She narrowed her eyes. "Don't make me waste my time reminding you of council proceedings. You know the drill, Nate."

Nate! Not only was the mayor on a first-name basis with the guy, they seemed to be downright familiar.

"Thanks, sis."

Casey and Hempstead locked eyes.

"Definitely an unexpected development, but nothing that can't be overcome," the attorney whispered in assurance.

Once again she turned to Cooper, who shrugged and held his palms upward.

"Will the spokesperson for Hearth and Home please take the speaker's stand?"

Before he rose and stepped to the mike, Hempstead gave Casey's arm a reassuring pat. It had the reverse effect he'd intended. She wanted to slap him silly for the condescending act.

Oh, Lord, have Your way in this situation today and don't allow me to do or say anything I'll regret.

Casey had to grudgingly admit the corporate

attorney did a decent albeit boring job of making introductions, stating the facts of Hearth and Home's commercial plan for the island and recapping the details of the artifact find.

"With all due respect to the Native American heritage of Galveston County, the materials uncovered yesterday were nothing of sufficient note to prevent my client from resuming the work schedule. We request permission to continue construction in accordance with all permits issued by the City of Galveston."

"Thank you, Mr. Hempstead." The mayor nodded.

There was no smile from the woman, no eye contact to give Casey even the least bit of encouragement. Was it possible for a few clay pots to throw the skids under a multimillion-dollar project?

"My turn, Your Honor?"

"Yeeeeees, Nate."

The city official's tone as she acknowledged her brother was difficult to interpret. Was she tired of accommodating him or simply resigned to it? Casey's gut churned.

The man approached the podium. Where his sister was a striking, silver-haired woman, professional in every way, her brother was costumed as if headed for a historical reenactment. He was dressed head to toe in crudely fashioned animal skins, and carried a longbow in his clenched fist.

When he communicated, there was no mistaking

his passion, though it was difficult to hold back a smile. Instead of addressing the room and making his case, the man began a lyrical chant. He danced in rhythm around the speaker's podium and raised his bow in defiance.

"Nathan." The Mayor interrupted her brother's trancelike state. "That's not even close to Karankawan. It's Sioux and you picked it up watching *Dances With Wolves,* so cut that out. You have four minutes left."

He gave up on his theatrics and motioned for someone in the back of the chamber to join him. Heads turned toward a small band of similarly dressed people sporting painted faces and feather headdresses. They made a compelling if out-of-place picture as they shuffled single-file down the center aisle.

A tall figure in a dark suit at the back of the room caught Casey's eye. Her heart lurched.

"Stick a fork in this deal. It's done," she mumbled.

Leaning against the far wall, seemingly engrossed in the proceedings, stood Barrett Westbrook. His arms were folded, his head cocked to one side, taking in the show.

His expression was grim. Like her future.

The bespectacled sergeant at arms spoke up, redirecting the room to matters of business.

"Our rules of order normally allow each of you five minutes at the podium. However, precedent has long ago been set on this particular issue and the council will only entertain one spokesperson from your *tribe* with your time commencing immediately."

A slight woman in beaded buckskins and thick black braids edged through the small group and adjusted the mike to her height. She addressed the officials, her words bearing a clipped Native American cadence.

"I am Little Conch, here to speak for a people unable to defend themselves. The peace-loving Karankawan survived untold centuries on this island only to be wiped out of existence by Anglo settlers a hundred and fifty years ago. The ground they trod is sacred and deserves to remain undisturbed. So many exceptions have already been made, so many discoveries plowed under and forgotten. We plead with this wise council to protect this find, to end the commercial expansion that daily chips away our heritage."

She stepped back, extended her arms and motioned for the others to follow. They formed a circle, facing inward as if shutting out the rest of the world. While the timer clicked off their remaining minutes they lowered their eyes and shared a mournful but enchanting song.

Casey was certain the language they used was none she'd ever heard before, but no translation was necessary to convey the sorrowful message. She felt a sudden conviction to do something to acknowledge their sadness, validate their need to represent the extinct tribe.

But what? Certainly there was something short of abandoning construction that would commemorate the find.

"Thank you, ladies and gentlemen." The mayor noted the end to their allotted time. "Before we adjourn to discuss the circumstances, would you like to say anything directly on behalf of your corporation, Miss Hardy?"

Unprepared to respond, Casey looked to the H & H legal counsel for guidance. Hempstead gave a slight shake of his head.

"No, thank you, Madam Mayor," she answered.

"There is no defense. That is why she will not speak," Nathan insisted.

Hempstead stood. "No *defense* is required and my client declines to be drawn into these theatrics. This is for the city to decide. Hearth and Home is a respected name built on the integrity of the Hardy family."

Emboldened, Nathan continued. "You heard 'em, sis. They think this is a sideshow instead of an effort to protect our home. And that's all the evidence you need to end this hostile takeover of our island by money-hungry outsiders here and now. Family business, my foot. Monkey business is more like it."

Casey pushed her chair back, preparing to stand. Beneath the table Hempstead signaled with his hand that she should stay put. He leaned close, spoke in a barely audible whisper.

"They want you to get up there so they can rattle you. These folks are nothing more than professional hecklers. Your father called us in for this purpose, so let me do my job."

How could she sit idly and leave this to a man she didn't know and couldn't trust while strangers impugned the Hardy name? Numbness surged into her hands. Her heart started to thump erratically against her ribs.

She sucked in a breath, and released it slowly. What could she say anyway? What words would refute their claims? Even if the syllables came to mind she knew she'd never be able to get them past her lips. Her mouth was dry as dust and her tongue felt like a lump of mud. Useless and dirty. She raised a trembling hand to loosen the collar of her silk blouse.

"Well then," the mayor said while standing. "If there's no more discussion—"

"Madam Mayor, if I may have a word." A voice carried from behind as Barrett made his way to the speaker's podium.

Casey's ribs ached from the frantic pounding inside her chest. Her lungs seized up, unable to expand and contract. What if she passed out from the sheer panic that was invading her? Did people *die* from the heebie-jeebies? Even if she survived physically, her career would be smothered before it had ever truly breathed on its own. Suffocated before all these prying, uncaring eyes. And it seemed an attorney would be her undoing after all.

Not Barrett! Please, Lord.

Not by the hand of the man I'm falling in love with, she admitted to herself as she pleaded with God.

Chapter Eleven

"You have five minutes, sir, commencing now."

"Thank you." Barrett bowed respectfully, first to the panel of officials and then to the table where Casey and her attorney were seated. He allowed his gaze to linger a moment on eyes bright with emotion that gripped his heart.

The woman was terror stricken. Paralyzed by another of her jeebie episodes. Would the observations he was about to make do Casey more harm than good? Maybe the best thing for everyone involved would be to take this stress off her shoulders and turn the project back over to her more experienced brother. A solution he knew would break her spirit. A spirit he was now certain he cared for deeply.

"Barrett Westbrook, of Westbrook Partners, Esquire. I must confess I feel somewhat ill-prepared to speak to such an illustrious panel of officials without my powdered wig and judicial robe." He intoned the apology in his most pompous voice and waited while the room rumbled with the laughter he'd hoped for. Americans seemed drawn to the accent of their mother tongue and he would stoop to any foolish trick to win over this small crowd.

"I represent a client who is considering a partnership agreement with Hearth and Home, so a quick resolution of this incident is of utmost interest to me. As much as I'm enjoying your unique brand of hospitality, I'd like to be on a flight to England in a couple days. Therefore I spent a rather sleepless night investigating the Native American folklore of South Texas for myself.

"As I also come from an island steeped in history, I appreciate the concerns expressed today over the safeguarding of your heritage." He gave an obsequious nod of his head toward the small band of oddly costumed individuals.

"However, I think it's also important to be accurate about the nature of that heritage. Just as some barbarous behavior has taken place on the British Isles over thousands of years on the part of her many rulers, it appears that a healthy dose of aggressive nature also existed among your Karankawan friends who—"

"Wait just a minute!" Nathan interrupted. "That tribe was a peace-loving bunch a folks who raised dogs and ate shellfish."

"Sir, the local crustaceans were not the only things

the Karankawan ate. They practiced tribal cannibalism, consuming bits of flesh of their dead and dying adversaries as the ultimate revenge."

"That was how they captured the enemy's courage," Nathan sputtered.

"Nate, one more outburst and I'll have you hauled out of the council chamber." The mayor admonished her brother. "Continue, Mr. Westbrook."

"My point is that we cannot canonize a people simply because they are extinct. Historical accuracy is as important as artifact and site preservation and in this case I believe Miss Hardy's ideas are appropriate and will overcome any objections to continuing construction."

He turned to Casey. "I know you've not yet confirmed all details, but may I outline your plan?"

A spark of cool control returned as her eyes narrowed and she leveled a look that was just short of a warning. But the small smile that curved her perfect lips said she'd go along, although she was clearly still suspicious, not certain she could trust him. His ego ached at the realization. He'd earn the woman's trust if it was the last thing he did. He turned to address the room.

"Hearth and Home is prepared to discontinue any further disturbance of the excavated area and to mark that ground and the immediate surroundings as a place of respect to all Native American tribes of Texas, but featuring the Karankawas. A life-size bronze depiction of the nomads who most likely camped there only very briefly will be the centerpiece of a peaceful park to be enjoyed by the island's residents and visitors."

The room erupted in applause and cheers of approval. The city councilmens' comments could be heard above the audience.

"Great solution!"

"It's about time!"

"Perfect gesture!"

Even the costumed protesters smiled as they squinted in concentration to visualize the scene.

"So much for that one little spot, but what about the way commercialism is constantly eating away at our island? What about that?" Nathan griped without making eye contact with his sister who looked as if she wanted to take her wooden gavel to his head.

"I think it's time you heard about the Hearth and Home plan for Galveston's crisis recovery." Barrett turned again to Casey, this time knowing she'd take the handoff without faltering. She didn't disappoint. With no thought for gaining approval, she brushed past the attorney at her table and moved to Barrett's side at the speaker's stand.

"I welcome the opportunity to share the H & H family vision for community support. Our corporate position has proven successful time and again. We invest in the lives of our employees and in the future of the communities we serve." Emboldened by the nods of agreement, Casey removed the microphone from the stand and moved from behind the podium.

As she warmed to her subject, Barrett watched Casey masterfully work the locals. Could this be the right woman to manage this deal, after all? If she could overcome her moments of panic, she would be an amazing partner for the right opportunity.

For the right man.

His spirits soared at the thought of being that man.

"Hearth and Home selected Galveston for a supercenter in spite of your vulnerability to violent weather. We bring the capacity to have an immediate impact on recovery from a crisis. In the event of a catastrophic storm like the hurricane that leveled this city a hundred years ago, we can tap into our resource network for the materials you will need for a large-scale recovery. That commitment will be our promise to you as a friend and employer in this community. My family is blessed to be a blessing to others and we take that commission literally."

Little Conch approached Casey until the two stood toe to toe. Actually it was moccasin to fancy high heel, which caused Barrett to bite the inside of his lip to prevent a smile during such a serious moment. But he'd seen so many strange and wonderful sights in his few days in Texas. What more did it have in store for him? He wanted to stay longer and find out.

But mostly, he wanted to be with Casey.

"My people have sought peace and friendship for ages. We ask only for the respect that those of all cultures are due. You are offering that to us, and I thank you."

She raised her hand toward Casey, giving up a token too small for Barrett to identify. Casey accepted the gift, closed her fingers then wrapped her arms around Little Conch. Something acutely personal passed between the two women in this public setting. When the brief exchange ended, Little Conch spoke again.

"Your Honor, we respectfully withdraw our objections to the Hearth and Home expansion and encourage the city to grant permission to continue construction."

The mayor glanced back and forth for any sign of objection, then removed her small pair of reading glasses and positioned them atop her head.

"I say we make quick work of resolving this so we can move on to the next agenda item. If there are no further speakers on the subject, the council hereby upholds all building permits and authorizes Hearth and Home to resume work. We will take a ten-minute recess and then return to the rest of the city's business."

While the occupants of the room broke into pockets of discussion and engaged Casey in conversation, Barrett approached the H & H attorney and offered his hand.

"Thanks for your intervention, Westbrook. From our briefing this morning I wasn't sure that young lady was going to cooperate. Right now she's a bit of a loose cannon, but with a few years of the right mentoring she'll be a dynamo."

"So, you think she lacks maturity?"

"She's still green, and seems to have a problem with handing over authority. If she doesn't take a step back and gain some perspective she'll be emotionally fried before she's forty."

"I've suggested she invest in a professional coach."

"How'd she take it?" A knowing smile deepened the creases in the older man's face.

"Just as you might expect," Barrett admitted.

And he also had to admit privately to himself that Casey's driven nature was a two-edged sword. It could be her recipe for success or her road map to destruction. He'd give her the benefit of the doubt in the blink of an eye regarding personal affairs. But did he dare take a professional chance on her?

"I wish your client much success. If they're going to partner with that one—" he angled his head toward Casey "—they need to buckle up for a wild ride."

The man collected his attaché, shook hands with Cooper and then left without speaking to Casey.

Barrett noticed the Ten Commandments prominently displayed on the wall of the council chamber. He dipped his chin and closed his eyes for a moment.

Father, I've struggled with so many decisions, always trusting You to guide my steps. This uncertainty about my career is a bit much and now I have the weight of Casey's to consider, as well. Please don't let her be hurt at my hand, and not at a time when she seems most vulnerable. Show me Your will and in all ways let it be done in my life.

"I should sucker punch you for interfering like that."

His eyes opened to bright yellow pointy toes, one of them tapping the floor before him. The shoes and the voice were distinctly those of the Warden. But the sparkling blue eyes that looked up into his face were pure Casey. Gone was the fear, though the bruise-like smudges beneath them gave away the fatigue that lingered. If the woman didn't get some stress relief and rest she was going to be a candidate for a collapse. No wonder she was on the fringe of panic attacks.

"Good morning to you, too, Casey. I didn't for a moment expect your undying gratitude. But neither did I anticipate physical threat as my reward for a marathon study on the failed efforts of European settlers to co-exist with Native Americans."

"Why didn't you tell me about this last night?"

"Because you'd have instructed me to mind my own business." He held his palm outward to block any interruption, then continued. "But the fact is that your business *is* my business. At least for as long as you continue to entertain any plan to work with my client. So I simply did my part to protect our mutual interest with or without your permission. Now, if it is still your intention to punish me, take your best shot."

He angled his chin and tapped his jaw with the tip of his finger and closed his eyes tightly as if anticipating impact.

To his delight, gentle lips pressed against the very spot he'd indicated as her target.

"Thank you, Barrett." Her voice was soft, sincere. "My independent streak is also my Achilles' heel. I've lost count of how many times in my life I've turned away help because it was more important to do things myself."

"I imagine the number is quite large," he couldn't resist saying.

She didn't deny it. "And my stubborn nature probably would have cost me dearly if you hadn't come to my rescue today. I'll never forget what you just did, even if you really were protecting other interests."

The amazing lady before him was the only other interest he wanted to protect. She was a woman he respected. Desired. Enjoyed.

Loved.

Casey watched the strangest expression sweep across Barrett's face, as if he'd suddenly discovered something important.

She opened her palm, extended it toward him and offered up the gift inside.

His dark eyes grew wide with interest and then softened as he recognized what lay in her hand. Being tossed about in the sea and sand had left the small pink shell dull, the colors muted. But etched deeply in the surface was the distinct outline of a fish. Casey reached into her jacket pocket and pulled out the coin Barrett had insisted she take the day before.

Their symbol of trust.

She placed it beside the shell in her palm.

"You gave me yours. Now you take mine."

"Oh, I couldn't." He shook his head and refused to accept the offering.

"Why not?"

"Mine is only a trinket, a die cast of scrap metal. What you have there is natural. One of a kind. And because it came from Little Conch it will always be of special significance to you."

She compared the two pieces that lay side by side. Though the shell was a wonder of nature, the mass-produced coin that Barrett had given as a sign of trust was the piece that made her chest tight with emotion.

With love.

"You carried this in your pocket as a reminder of your faith and that is what makes it meaningful to me. And if you hadn't intervened today—"

"I thought you said I interfered."

She refused to take his bait and be distracted.

"If you hadn't intervened on my behalf today we might not have come to the conclusion that caused Little Conch to share this with me."

She took his hand and carefully uncurled his fingers. The cuts were healing nicely, doing so much better after only a few days of Texas sunshine and the warm sea air. She placed the shell across his life line and pressed her palm to his. Warmth passed between them, electric in its intensity.

"Please, Barrett. Take it."

His gaze was fixed on hers. The expression from a few minutes earlier was back. Crinkles radiated from the outside corners of his eyes. It could have been aggravation, confusion or even agreement. The man was impossible to read.

"Miss Casey, you ready to go?" Cooper stood a discreet distance away.

She withdrew from the comfort of their innocent contact and stepped toward the table to gather her belongings.

"Go ahead, sir," Barrett said to Cooper. "Casey's riding with me. I'll escort her back to her home."

"Perfect," she agreed. "Then I can change and head straight over to the site to make sure everybody's called to the job and we're back on track."

"Cooper, would you be kind enough to handle that today so your boss lady can get some rest? To be blunt, she doesn't appear to have slept well, if at all."

Her head snapped up at his take-charge manner. Normally she'd construe such comments as fighting words. But she had to admit he was dead right. If she didn't get some REM sleep soon she was going into a full-blown meltdown the next time the stress level cranked up.

"Truth be told, Mr. Westbrook, that's actually my job. Miss Casey likes to tell me how to do it, but she usually knows what she's talkin' about so I don't object. Much."

"Now hear this." Casey cupped her hands around

her mouth, megaphone-style. "You're both right. Enjoy the moment because it may never happen again. Cooper, I'm getting out of your hair for the rest of today."

"And tomorrow," Barrett added.

Her hands fell limp at her sides as the hope in his eyes made her heart beat at double time. What did he have in mind? Business or pleasure?

Wake up and smell the prison chow before it's too late, Warden.

She could hear her brother's voice, encouraging her to let up on the gas. To take some time to enjoy life and the salary piling up in her bank account.

She'd known he was right, but she'd always believed there was plenty of time for that. She was young and had at least thirty-five work years ahead of her. What would a couple of days away from the job matter?

Especially when the man she loved would be gone by the weekend.

Gone.

Back to life on another continent with her dreams and now her heart in his hands.

Chapter Twelve

A blast of cool air welcomed Casey back into the condo. She dropped down to the sofa, eased off her Manolo's and positioned the outrageously expensive heels on the low coffee table. Her gaze fell on the Bible and concordance still open from her late-night study. How nice it would be to take refuge in the Word and give up the pressures of her job for a while. Maybe Barrett was on to something.

"There's *nothing* in your fridge but diet soda," Barrett called from her kitchen. "What on earth do you do when you get hungry in the middle of the night?"

"Drink a Fresca and pop a couple of breath mints."

"No wonder you're so thin."

"You sound like Savannah."

"Since I find your girl Friday to be exceedingly competent and resourceful, I shall take that as a compliment."

Casey had to smile at the muffled quality of Barrett's voice. His head was buried in the pantry in search of food. He'd offered to take her out to lunch but she'd declined. It took effort to keep her eyes open. She couldn't afford to add "falling asleep face-first in her soup" to the long list of shortcomings amassing against her.

Ice rattled in a glass in the next room where he'd evidently made himself at home. Amazing how he'd acclimated in the few days since his arrival. The stuffy, demanding stranger who'd appeared on Monday had morphed into a casual, helpful friend.

Friend?

Yes, he'd become a friend. But she wanted so much more from him. She wanted Barrett for her best friend. For her soul mate. For her love.

She leaned her head against the cushion and closed her eyes. She heard his footsteps cross the tiled kitchen floor then become muted by the thick carpet. A glass clinked as he set her cold drink on the table.

"Don't fall asleep quite yet," he instructed. He gave her shoulder a soft nudge. "Take my hand. I'll help you up. Go get out of your suit and into your bed so you can rest comfortably."

She opened her eyes, once again shocked by the realization that she had the personal attention of this attractive man. Of course, there was still the chance that the primary objective of that attention was to confirm she was out like a light so he could resume his work. Work that would decide her fate.

Suddenly a nap didn't sound like a wise idea. She needed to keep an eye on him.

"Nope." She shook her head and swiped at the hand he offered. "I can't justify going back to bed in broad daylight when I'm not sick."

"Sick is precisely what you will be if you don't get some sleep."

He grasped her hand and tugged, as if hauling her to her feet took no effort at all. Turning her about-face, he gave her a push toward the hallway.

"I'll lock the door from the inside when I see myself out."

"No, don't." She shook off fatigue. She had to distract him from his mission.

"Don't lock the door?"

"Don't leave," she almost pleaded.

He smiled, kindness filling his eyes.

"But you need to rest, my sweet Casey."

Oddly, neither the tone nor the endearment made her feel patronized. Coming from Barrett, it was comforting. And for that reason she wanted him to stay. She wanted him near. She desired his presence, if only for the days that were left.

"I need your company more. Stay for a while longer. Please, Barrett."

"As you wish."

Gratitude washed over her like a sudden, unexpected rain shower. When had she become so needy?

Instead of continuing on to her bedroom to change,

she turned back to Barrett, stepped close and wrapped her arms around him. He hesitated ever so slightly before encircling her in his embrace. He pulled her tight, tucked her head beneath his chin and released a long breath from deep inside.

"Casey, bear with me, please. I have no idea where God will lead this but I have a clear notion of where I hope it will go. Like all of Texas, this is uncharted territory for me. I have to find my way slowly so I won't make a mistake and forget my purpose for being here."

With her ear pressed to his chest, the hard thumping of his heart was impossible to ignore. But his words were equally undeniable. The man was seeking his purpose, his role within the family who'd given him education, opportunity and trust. He wouldn't let anything overshadow that. Realizing he loved his family as deeply as she loved hers only served to make her want him more.

And instead of doing what her heart desired, tipping her face up to ask for his kiss, she whispered, "I understand completely," and then made her way to her room to change.

The door clicked shut behind Casey and Barrett shot both hands through his hair to rest on the back of his neck. What would Sig have to say about all this? Would he laugh his fool head off over this unpredictable affair of the heart and say "I told you so"? Would he encourage his Oxford chum to enjoy the moment and not expect too much from it? Or would he admonish Barrett to keep his eye on the ball, get the job done and get out of Dodge?

Dodge?

My word, I'm starting to think like a cowboy! This place is wearing off on me!

He picked up the icy drink he'd prepared for Casey and drank it down as if that would extinguish the wildfire growing inside his heart. Before he put the first word of a recommendation on the page he knew instinctively he was in a no-win situation. Not only was there no way to win, there was certainly heartache to be found. He hadn't kept relationships to the surface all these years to let things get out of hand now. And in Texas of all places. The last location on earth where he had any reason to be for more than a few days tops.

He needed to return to the solid cliffs of Tintagel to regain his perspective. Everything he valued, everything he loved was in England.

Everything…but Casey.

"I know you want to leave, but would you sit with me for a while? Just until I doze off?"

Where an accomplished female executive had passed through the doorway only moments before, not much more than a girl stood now. Dressed in an Iowa State Cyclones T-shirt and baggy jeans, Casey padded toward him on feet covered by striped red-and-green socks. Beneath her arm she carried a blanket and pillow as if headed for a primary school sleepover.

"Of course I will," he agreed, unable to refuse her.

He took the bedding and stretched it over the comfy sofa, positioning the pillow at the far end. When she settled into the deep cushions and pulled the blanket up to her chin, colorful toes popped out the bottom. He removed the daily news from a Queen Anne side chair and prepared to take a seat.

She shook her head. "Not there, over here. With me." She patted the sofa. "I feel the shivers coming on and that's a bad sign. When this used to happen before Savannah would hold my feet in her lap and that helped me fall asleep."

The quiver in her voice was barely perceptible, but he heard it.

"Would you mind?"

"Not even the least bit," he assured her. "In fact, a close encounter with Pippi Longstocking has always been my secret wish."

She pulled her knees to her body, making room for him to sit then stretched her legs so her feet barely grazed his thigh.

"Oh, do stop playing chicken."

Hoping to ease her obvious discomfort he grabbed Casey's ankles, tugged her closer so her heels rested in his lap and then began to massage her soles with the pads of his thumbs.

She brought her hands from beneath the cover and pushed it to her waist but continued to clutch her fingers together as if to prevent them from trembling. Her sleepy gaze was almost sad, filled with apology.

"Close your eyes," he instructed.

She complied, a weak moan escaping with her breath. The sound of longing threw him off balance, much as her unexpected hug had before. As he worked the stress out of her feet he chatted to normalize the unusual closeness that was settling between them.

"Did you know that the lines on the bottom of your feet were developed before you were born?"

"Huh?" Her eyes fluttered halfway open.

"It's a stamp of individuality, just like a fingerprint."

"I think I've heard that," she muttered as her lids drooped.

"And the sole of the foot is covered by the most dense skin on your body."

"That so?" The two syllables barely made it past her lips. Beautiful lips he wanted desperately to kiss.

"Yes." He kept up the unnecessary rambling. "The pressure of our weight makes the skin thickest there."

No comment.

"Casey?"

No response. Her breathing had grown slow, steady and deep. He reached his hand to cover hers. The skin was cool where the blood had left her extremities. Probably part of the physical symptom that she said caused her hands to tingle. As his warmth enveloped her, she stirred a bit in her sleep. The tension in her hands abated, her grip relaxed and something fell from her grasp, rolling to the sofa and then bouncing to the floor. Barrett leaned to get a look at what she'd been holding so tightly.

There on the carpet lay his coin with the fish symbol stamped into it.

Casey's neck hurt and her nose was mashed against something itchy. In the distance there was singing and a wonderful smell. Tentatively, she cracked one eye open. The room was dark. Rolling over, she looked for her bedside clock and the bottom dropped out from under her. Arms flailed as she grabbed for security.

"What the—" Her comment was cut off by a resounding *whump* as her backside made contact with the hard floor.

"Ow!"

She kicked at the blanket that had her pinned between the legs of the sofa and the coffee table.

The overhead light blazed and she squinted against it.

"Good evening, Sleeping Beauty. You must be famished."

Either an angel or Barrett loomed above her with a halo of light surrounding his head. Undeterred, she squirmed to free herself from the cocoon.

"Be still and let me assist." Humor laced his voice. He moved the table back a foot and squatted to untangle her legs from the duvet. Once she was free, he took hold of both hands and pulled her upright.

"There. Good as new," he pronounced.

She twisted to take in her surroundings, finally re-membering falling asleep on the couch. And from the crick in her neck, she'd been there for quite a while.

"What time is it and what are you still doing here?" she snapped.

He ignored her rudeness and turned back toward the kitchen. As he walked away, he slung a white dish towel over his shoulder.

"It's almost eight and I've left and come back twice. It took two trips to find everything I needed to prepare this meal, so you'd best eat every morsel. Savannah, you may open the shades now that Her Majesty has arisen."

"Hey, girl!" Savannah called. "Glad you woke up in time to join us. We'd decided to give you fifteen more minutes, then start without you."

"I'm sorry I held you two up from your hot dinner date."

Savannah poked her head through the serving win-dow that connected the kitchen to the dining area.

"For a lady who's been drooling in her sleep the whole day while her two friends have shopped, chopped and grilled, you're a little on the grouchy side." She held up a chip covered with chunky guaca-mole and prepared to pop it into her mouth. "Go get your hair under control and then come see what we've whipped up. I guarantee it'll put you in a better mood."

Casey ducked her chin, letting wild locks cover her face as well as her embarrassment. Okay, she *was* being cranky but the whole situation was awkward and griping just seemed like the best way to handle it. Maybe she should gather up her pillow and blanket and call it a night instead of making the effort with dinner companions.

Barrett returned carrying a chilled mug of lemonade and a serving tray piled high with coarsely chopped *Pico de Guio* and blue corn chips. The aroma of cilantro and diced tomatoes turned Casey's empty stomach into a noisy beggar.

Barrett smiled, clearly pleased with her tummy's uncontrollable reaction.

"That's the affirmation every chef hopes for. Care to join us on the patio?"

She accepted the glass, eagerly shoveled in a scoop of fresh salsa and spoke with her mouth full.

"Ooh, this is heavenly." She grabbed a couple more chips and moved toward the hallway. "Just give me a few minutes and I'll be right there. Don't start without me," she called as she locked herself inside the bathroom and turned to the vanity mirror.

The creature who stared back was right out of a horror flick. Medusa spirals shot in every direction and for the second time that day the imprint of the sofa was embossed across her nose and cheek. She looked like Freddie Krueger on a bad hair day! She splashed her face with cool water to rinse off dried saliva— Savannah hadn't been joking—and squirted Visine into itchy eyes.

"Oh my goodness," she complained.

"Did you see the flowers from the Cartel?" Savannah's voice carried into the bathroom.

"What are you talking about?" Casey asked as she opened the door and let her friend slip inside.

"In your bedroom." Savannah pointed toward the master suite. "There's a huge arrangement of yellow roses from the Cartel. Doc brought them by to congratulate you on swinging the city council vote to resume construction."

"Oh, great!" Casey squeezed her eyes tight and pressed the heels of her hands to her temples. "So I looked like roadkill in front of my construction partners as well as the man of my dreams."

"The man of your dreams, huh?"

Casey covered her mouth. "Did I say that out loud?"

"You certainly did." Savannah smiled her approval and moved to the far side of the garden-style bathroom where they were less likely to be overheard. She settled on the edge of the deep marble tub and motioned for her friend to provide details. "So, tell."

Casey hung her head, not sure where to start.

"That bad, huh?"

"The worst."

"You're really taken with him, aren't you?"

She raised her eyes knowing she couldn't hide the tears of overwhelming emotion that had pooled and were ready to spill over.

"Oh, my!" Her friend mouthed the words.

"I've never known anything like this. Never believed it was even possible to feel so strongly in such a short time." She put her hands over her face, hiding her eyes even as she exposed the truth.

"No wonder your attacks are back."

"Oh, Savannah, what am I gonna do?" she whispered. "I've fallen head over heels with a man who is my worst nightmare personified."

Chapter Thirteen

How on earth had she allowed this to happen? Let her guard down low enough to come under the spell of a man who could and would wield power over her future with the stroke of his fancy fountain pen. A man who belonged to a profession that had rightly earned the skepticism of mankind in general and certainly hers in particular. And worse still, a man who would return to the home and life he loved in just a couple more days.

A life that was an ocean and a world away.

What would her father say when he heard that she'd been bailed out that morning by Barrett? More importantly, how could he trust the daughter who'd spent her life campaigning to oversee Hearth and Home once he discovered she'd crossed the line between professional and personal behavior? Everything she held most dear was in jeopardy.

And until today she hadn't known that at greatest risk of all was her own heart.

It had never been broken because she'd never exposed it. Now it seemed heartache was imminent and she was helpless to prevent it.

Sisterly arms encircling Casey, the two leaned forehead to forehead as Savannah began to pray.

"Abba Father, You promise that when we are in relationship with You we can trust in Your timing, trust in Your perfect plan. You reveal Your will for our lives as we seek You and we come together, seeking You now.

"Casey is hurting, Lord, and for the first time in forever she's confused about which way to turn. There's so much more at stake here than just her work. She's opened her heart and she's unsure of the consequences. She's been my lifelong friend and I know anyone Casey takes close, she treasures with all her being. Nothing short of true love will make her whole. So, Father, if it's Your will for this new relationship to blossom into something everlasting, we ask You to reveal Your plan and give my sister peace and purpose for her future."

"Amen and amen," they chorused.

Casey reached for a tissue to blow her nose. "How am I going to confess all this to my family?"

"Honey, you're a grown woman and you haven't done anything that requires or needs confessing. Just take this one day at a time and see where it goes."

"But I only have a couple more days, period."

"Then go make the most of them but keep a cool head. Enjoy the hours you have left together. From what I've witnessed he's already had a healthy dose of unvarnished Casey, so drop the Warden act with the man and just go be a woman."

"But what about the heebie-jeebies? I think I might be allergic again."

"Huh?"

"You know, allergic to Barrett. Ever since he showed up I've been on the verge of a full-blown attack. That hasn't happened since our junior year at Iowa State when I was dating that creep, Howard. Remember how we figured out that it had something to do with a physiological reaction to him?"

"Silly girl." Savannah petted Casey's head. "I just said that to make you feel better about dumping the jerk. You were in a caustic relationship and you were carrying a very heavy academic load at the same time. The guy was a loser. You were determined to turn him around and it ate away all your self-confidence when you couldn't make it happen. The only way to get you over it was to get you out of it."

"So you made all that stuff up about studying it in psych class?"

"Yep. Pretty good, huh?" She winked, obviously proud of the deception.

"I can't believe I fell for a story like that."

"Yeah, well that *story* and a year's worth of Prozac

got you through a rough patch. If you need to say you're allergic to Barrett, I'll go along with that, too. But I think it's just the opposite this time. Deep down inside, you think this man could be exactly what you want, but the place and the time may be all wrong. Only God knows the answers and He's always right."

"Thanks for your love and prayers, but I still don't know what I'm going to do." Casey pulled Savannah close again, so grateful for their friendship. So desperate for guidance.

"You're going to wait *patiently* and see what God reveals in the coming days."

The chiming of the doorbell caused the two to jump.

"Finish freshening up. I'll get the door."

Casey grabbed an orange tank top from her closet. She brushed her teeth and then twisted her hopeless hair into a chignon with no effort to subdue the twangers that sprang free.

"Ready or not, here I come."

Barrett was speechless at the sight Casey made when she joined them on the patio. She was refreshed and rested, the darkness above her cheekbones had faded. Her sparkling eyes were alight with emotion, her hair caught up in a beguiling way that took his breath. She'd changed into a blouse that revealed tanned and toned arms from the weeks of working shoulder to shoulder with her laborers. The woman wouldn't shy away from anything difficult, not hard work and not tough situations. Perhaps she was prepared to handle the demands of the job, after all.

"Howdy, young lady," Cooper greeted her from his seat at the outdoor table.

She took a chair and Barrett was pleased to see her fill a plate with the grilled potato and steak he'd just taken off the barbecue.

"I hope I didn't wake you when I called, but I wanted to drop this by." Cooper placed a thick legal-size packet on the glass surface between them.

"I was so far gone that I never heard the phone," she replied casually enough but leaned away from the envelope as if it were a scorpion.

"We could barely hear the ringing ourselves over the racket," Barrett quipped.

"Racket?"

"You were snoring like a bullfrog with adenoid problems." Savannah grinned at Barrett.

"Thank you, both, for your observations and for making me comfortable in my own home."

"It's a gift," Savannah announced as she spread a napkin across her lap. "We've already blessed the food so bon appétit."

"What's this, Coop?" Casey nudged the packet beside her place mat.

"Take a look."

"I'd rather not. It seems lawyerly, so you do it."

She cocked an eyebrow at Barrett who winked to reassure her that not all *lawyerly* things were bad.

"Suit yourself." Cooper dug into his meal, ignoring the envelope she scooted his way. "But I thought it was important to give you this news tonight. That, and I couldn't pass up a rare steak with my name on it."

He shaved off a large chunk of beef and chewed with gusto while Casey held her breath to hear what was so vital. When he reached for the steak sauce and busied himself with a stubborn cap she lost patience.

"Coop!"

"Oh, sorry." He grinned and feigned apology. "Don't fret. It's good news. The city loved your plan to build a park dedicated to Native Americans and they're offering to assist with funding as long as you employ local artists and craftsmen. During our grand opening they want to do a whole tourism campaign around your idea."

Barrett watched the muscles in Casey's jaw tense as she gritted her teeth.

"Is that strip hard to chew, Casey? I tenderized it myself." Savannah must have noticed, as well.

"The steak's wonderful. It's taking credit for that park idea that's impossible to swallow." She returned her fork and knife to the place mat, her food no longer of interest. "Barrett came up with the suggestion and he deserves the credit."

She looked toward the spot where he leaned against the balustrade to catch the warm evening breeze on his skin.

"We all know you pulled that meeting out of the fire

today." Casey was determined to give Barrett the credit he was due.

"It's not as dramatic as all that." He brushed off the accolade with a wave of his hand. "If there had been time to consider all the possibilities, you likely would have come to the same conclusion. And in fairness to you, after being advised to depend upon your legal representation, you did so. If, instead, you'd armed yourself with the same information I found, I'm confident the outcome would have been similar."

"Maybe so, but you not only came up with a win-win solution, you also handed me the perfect opportunity to announce our community crisis plan—"

"And that's what *really* swayed the council," Savannah interrupted.

"She's right," Cooper agreed.

Casey nodded, as if seeing the truth in what her friends said. She picked up a fork and dipped it into her stuffed baker before continuing.

"And so, Barrett, I want to go on record in front of these witnesses that I owe you the favor of your choice for helping us out of a difficult spot today. All you have to do is name it. Nothing reasonable is off-limits." She raised the food to her lips.

"Done," he announced as he pushed away from the railing, pleased that she'd laid her own snare.

"I'm cashing in my rain check. Go sailing with me tomorrow."

Casey's utensil dropped from her hand, clattered on

the surface of her plate, chipping the edge the smallest bit. Her reaction chipped away at Barrett's heart, as well. She was going to refuse him. She was about to show her true colors and take back her pledge. He steeled himself to make light of her rejection.

"Sorry about that." She grinned. "That potato was hotter than I expected." She took a sip of her drink, either to cool her lips or to buy time. Barrett's chest ached as he waited for her response.

"I should get back to work tomorrow. There's a lot to do to set this new project in motion if we're going to hit our grand opening deadline. But…" She scooped up more of her baker, blew on it and closed her eyes as she savored the taste.

"But?" He dared to hope. He wanted nothing more than to spend his last day in Texas alone with the woman he loved. He had to find a way to tell her, to show her.

Before it was too late.

"But there's no place I'd rather be than pitching about in a sailboat with you. What time will you pick me up?"

Barrett was still awake anticipating the day ahead with Casey when his cell phone trilled. A glance at the display window caused him to sit upright in his plush hotel bed. He stared at the tiny screen, unsure he cared to hear the voice on the other end of the line. While he considered how to handle the caller, the phone chirped a second, a third, then a fourth time and finally went silent. He tossed the phone aside. Whatever it was, it could wait. He'd deal with it on the weekend when he got home, if at all.

A red light began to flash, indicating a new voice message.

"Drat."

He reached for the aggravating instrument. Instinct said let it go, but it had to be something of importance to require contact at six in the morning, London time.

He pressed the playback key.

"Barrett, it's Caroline. I'm sorry to bother you, my darling, but Sigmund said you're out of the country and I felt certain you'd welcome a familiar accent." She paused to laugh, as if she'd said something humorous. "How rich that you're in Texas given the way you feel about the States."

He held down the pause button as a pang of remorse shot through him. He'd been so judgmental before, so smugly confined to his safe little world. So certain that all things familiar were evidence of all things perfect. He'd been completely and utterly wrong, unable to see another side or consider another option.

No wonder he'd been a failure at his trade.

He took a moment to give praise for the revelation.

Lord, thank You for pushing me out of the boat into the deep. I believe I'm finally beginning to see my future take shape and You've promised I can do all things through Christ who strengthens me.

He released the key so the message could continue.

"If you'll agree, I'd like to meet your flight. I've made a terrible mistake—"

She stopped so abruptly that he looked at the phone to see if the connection had been broken.

"Barrett, the truth is I was wrong about Andre and we won't be seeing one another again. Mostly, well, because I miss you. If you'll have me back I'll come under any terms. I'd rather have part of your heart than none at all. I won't demand more than you're prepared to give, you have my word.

"Very well then, I've said it. Do be a dear and text me your itinerary so I can hire a car for the trip out to Gatwick. I know you're not keen on hearing the words, Barrett, but I do care for you. I care very much."

The message ended and he activated the delete function. There was no need to listen again. The crossroad he'd always longed for, the moment of finding his purpose was looming in the immediate distance. It was time to make choices that would dictate the rest of his life. As confused and desperate as he'd been only days before, he was equally so now but for vastly different reasons.

Where his future had been without promise there was now bright possibility.

Where he'd refused to make decisions for his life there were now choices that demanded action.

Where there had been a relationship that seemed to be going nowhere, there was now at least one that could go anywhere.

He climbed off the bed, pulled a robe over his pajamas and moved into the sitting room. He needed the one thing that was in short supply. The one thing that was running out and couldn't be replaced.

Time.

He slipped his cell phone from the pocket of the pink hotel robe, pressed a programmed key and waited for the transatlantic connection. What was there to say? How honest was he prepared to be and what was the point in phoning otherwise?

The point was to buy time, if only a day or two.

"Hello?" The connection was made.

Barrett hesitated.

"Yes, hello, is anyone there?"

"Good morning."

"Son! How are you?"

Barrett's heart immediately felt lighter at the sound of his father's voice. He wasn't sure what the outcome of the conversation would be but he knew he'd made the right decision to phone.

"Very well, Father, all things considered."

"I trust the Lone Star State hasn't gotten the better of you," he joked.

"Not entirely, though there have been moments when I suspected the cuisine might."

They shared a chuckle and then his father got straight to the point.

"So, fill me in on how the discovery is going with Hearth and Home."

There it was. The opportunity to reveal all, to tell what he'd learned about himself and his fit within the firm. Here was the chance to ask for confirmation of his intentions. Even so, as close as Barrett felt he was to a final recommendation, there were still unanswered questions. If he exposed all he knew to his father now, what would the reaction be if he had a change of direction?

A change of heart?

"Jolly good, actually. It's been quite an enlightening visit with more than a few surprises. Not at all what I'd expected."

"In a positive way, I trust."

"Oh, yes. The team here has accommodated me far beyond expectations."

"Smashing news. Your mum will enjoy a nice 'I told you so' when you return. Now, tell me your impression of Guy Hardy? He has a stellar reputation."

"That's one of the surprises I mentioned. Mr. Hardy only recently stepped down from his position to be replaced by another family member."

"I respect your judgment, Barrett. If you're confident the replacement is equally adept, we're prepared to move forward as soon as you return."

Casey was certainly qualified for many challenges, but the jury was still out—he smiled at his lame pun—where a final decision was concerned.

"I presume you will make it back on your scheduled flight."

"That's the plan, but I might need to delay a bit." Barrett set the stage to draw things out a while longer.

"Given your deliberate nature, I don't need to tell you to take your time. But we'd dearly love to have you back for your mum's birthday celebration. The entire family will be here."

"Oh, yes." Barrett thumped himself in the forehead with the heel of his hand. How could he have forgotten. Of course he couldn't delay. And, really, it was best to get on with it anyway. No point in putting off the inevitable. "Count on seeing me for sure then."

"Will the beautiful Caroline be joining us, as well? It's about time you two made this courtship official, don't you think?"

Barrett's insides twisted as if a fist tightly gripped his gut. He'd only confided the embarrassing breakup to Sigmund, knowing his friend could be trusted with a private matter. But family, even the most discreet members who were professionally sworn to confidentiality, were likely to gossip.

And what was the answer to his father's question anyway? A week ago he'd fancied his relationship with Caroline had been on solid ground even if not a head-over-heels experience that filled the pages of paperback novels. And today he believed himself in love with a woman he'd only just met, an emotion that went against his very grain.

Was it better to be a public fool for love or a private one for convenience?

"I'm sorry. From your silence I can tell it's none of my concern."

"Not true, Father. It's just that at the moment I can't speak to your questions because I don't have the answers."

"Ah…"

Barrett could imagine the silver head nodding, appreciating even if not fully understanding the dilemma.

"My boy, a fork in the path is to be expected in life. But it often produces growth and builds character, so don't wish it away. Pray for discernment and let your mum and me know if we can help with your choices."

Barrett closed his eyes and let his head fall back against the leather sofa. George Elliot had said, "It's our choices that show what we are, far more than our abilities."

What would his choices ultimately say about him to his God, to his family, to the woman he loved?

Chapter Fourteen

The prospect of seeing Casey turned Barrett's insides to mint jelly. He was a young boy again, unable to find the words to express the powerful tugging at his heartstrings. In the night he'd awakened several times, replayed Caroline's message in his memory, considered the words of his father, searched his spirit for honest intentions and prayed for clarity.

His conclusion was the same each time; the Heavenly Father had brought Barrett to this place and this moment intentionally. But the question remained whether the intent was identifying his role in the family or finding the love of his life.

The options seemed to be at cross-purposes.

As shards of light began to streak the sky through the window of his suite, anticipation for the day ahead had him fidgeting. He drummed his fingers on the rim of his empty coffee cup and stared at the notes on the table before him. The list of pros and cons was beginning to paint an undeniable picture, taking a form that couldn't be ignored. How was he going to put this decision aside long enough to enjoy what might be his last day with his lady love? And if he succeeded in pushing business to the back of his mind, how would he ever come to the right conclusion?

It would be a test of his patience as well as his strength. Forty years of life had given him some measure of maturity. If only he could harness it today and conduct himself like a man deserving of the degrees and licenses hanging on his office wall. He'd never truly felt like that pedigreed individual and today was no exception. How could one have a career built on evidence and then for something as unstable and unpredictable as love let intelligence swirl down the plug hole?

Love.

He was in love.

His temples throbbed in time with the beating of his heart as his insides churned. The cacophony of conflicting symptoms was as painful as it was joyful. He glanced down at his chest, certain the pounding could be seen through his clothes. He was relieved to see the soft knit of his navy collared shirt lying flat, undisturbed.

"It's a good job I'm off this island and out of this state tomorrow. I'm too old for these physical sensations. Surely they'll pass as quickly as they overtook me."

But as he spoke the words out loud he knew beyond a reasonable doubt he was wrong.

* * *

"You are such a doofus," Savannah announced as she breezed through the room carrying a laundry basket.

Casey let the curtain fall back into place and stepped away from the window. She'd been strategically positioned to keep an eye on the parking lot without being seen from outside for nearly an hour.

"What?" She feigned ignorance.

"Oh, save the round-eyed innocence for Barrett. I saw you over there like a guard in the watchtower. The prisoner will be here any minute, Warden, so come eat your breakfast."

"That obvious, huh?" Casey followed instructions and moved into the kitchen where her untouched meal waited on the island.

"Why do you bother trying to hide your feelings from me after all these years?" Savannah propped her basket on one knee and slid back the louver that concealed a small laundry space. "And more importantly, why do you still deny them yourself?"

Casey perched on the tall stool and toyed with her cottage cheese and berries. Her friend had asked a simple question. Too bad there wasn't an easy answer.

"Will you settle for an 'I don't know'?"

"Will you?" Savannah dumped powdered detergent into the machine, spun a dial and closed the lid. She turned, folded her arms and leaned against the washer. "Will you go on pretending that making your daddy proud and making your brother eat your dust is what life is all about? Even now that you know for certain there's a better reason than a big-box store to get up in the morning?"

"That's not fair," Casey protested.

"Forget fair. It won't be fair when Barrett takes off tomorrow and you're alone again. But it'll be reality. I hope all that ambition of yours will be good company. Giving up the best chance you may ever have for happiness is a high price to pay for success."

Casey shoved her bowl away and dropped her face into her hands. What had been excitement moments earlier was turning to dread.

"Savannah, I've had my career mapped out forever. Of all people, you can't possibly expect me to put it aside just because a man I've known for a few days has gotten under my skin," Casey insisted. Even as she spoke the words she knew the argument was a waste of time. Still, she had to at least make the effort. If she couldn't convince her best friend she knew the right path to take, how could she convince herself?

"Have it your way, but there's a reason why the heebie-jeebies are back and I don't believe it has anything to do with allergies or stress. You feel threatened by Barrett and you have since the moment he drove onto the lot. He has some authority you can't control. And now, whether he knows it or not, he has power over your heart. He's determined to make an informed decision about the business. For heaven's sake, honey, don't let him fly blind about the personal."

"What are you suggesting?" She raised her head, hoping to glean some wisdom.

Savannah stepped to the opposite side of the countertop and leaned down so they were elbow to elbow, eye to eye.

"I'm not suggesting, I'm saying it outright. You've always seized opportunity. And you've never shied away from tough situations that called for the truth. Tell that man you care before it's too late. He needs to hear the words you said to me last night. If you let him leave without taking that chance, you will second guess yourself for the rest of your life."

"You think so?"

"I know so."

"Allow me, Casey."

Barrett stepped behind her and gave a sharp tug to tighten the life preserver strap. He turned her to face him and straightened the orange vest that was puffed up around her chin.

"Much better," he assessed, then placed a reassuring hand to the small of her back as he steered her toward the dock.

His voice was so calm, so full of patience. But somehow it only made Casey more ill at ease. He'd been treating her like an unpredictable child or a skittish animal since she'd greeted him at her door an hour earlier. Was she that obvious, that pitiful?

"Does it need to be so tight?" she complained, slipping her hand beneath the flotation device to ease the tension against her ribs.

"Only if you want it to function properly in the event we capsize."

"What are the odds of that?"

He tipped his head back to study the morning sky. It was clear of clouds, a pallet of blue streaked with a hundred hues of red, orange and yellow. A watercolor masterpiece from God's own hand.

"You can count on a warm spray but the chances of taking a dip this morning are slim to none. All you need to do is follow instructions and relax while somebody else takes the helm."

She came to an abrupt stop at the edge of the boardwalk and refused to budge.

"You, Savannah and Cooper. If another person tells me to loosen up I'm going to turn around and go back to the condo."

"Not a chance, Miss Hardy." Barrett stepped onto the wooden planks, slipped his hands beneath her arms and lifted her effortlessly up to join him. Instead of moving away he pulled her nearer, pressed her life vest to his and brought his face close. He hovered above her, their eyes mere inches apart.

"You will not get away from me without a struggle. I intend to have you near me for as long as possible." His voice was husky.

"Until tomorrow, you mean." She needed perspective.

"I mean what I said. For as long as possible."

His lips met hers. The urgency of his kiss was undeniable. A rush of pleasure surged as she closed her eyes and molded perfectly into his arms. The plastic puffiness between them squeaked as she pressed her palms to his back, pulling him as close as the decency of broad daylight permitted.

Certain they were becoming a source of interest at the busy marina, Casey prudently loosened her hold on Barrett and withdrew from the ardent kiss. Still, he was close enough for his breath to be a whisper against her cheek.

"Barrett, my world has flipped over on its edge since the moment you parked that land yacht on my property last Monday."

"That confession gives me great comfort," he murmured.

"Then why don't I feel the same? Instead of peace there's a swarm of helplessness buzzing in my head. A revelation like this should fill me with joy, not scare me to death."

"A revelation like what?"

Tension hummed between them as he waited for her answer.

She couldn't see his face, could only imagine the darkened intensity of his eyes as his cheek pressed close to hers.

Could she say it? Did she dare? Savannah was right. This might be her only chance. It was not in her DNA to let it slip past without grasping for the prize. She had to speak the words, especially while he couldn't see her face.

"I love you," she breathed, relieved to have the secret out.

A silent moment passed.

"Beg pardon?"

"You're joking, right?" There was no way she'd laid her heart bare and he hadn't heard.

"No, sorry." He raised his head, looked down into her face with an apologetic smile. "Your curls were against my ear and I didn't catch what you said. Tell me again about this revelation."

Maybe it was a sign. She'd said the wrong thing and mercifully been given a do-over.

Then Guy's words came back to her. On the day he'd shared his decision to wed he'd cautioned his baby sister not to be blinded by ambition, not to forget what mattered most in life. Hadn't Savannah said as much today when she'd warned Casey against waiting until it was too late to speak her feelings?

She searched the sparkling eyes above hers for encouragement. What she saw reflected emboldened her. She placed a palm on either side of his face and drew him in until the depths of his eyes and the invitation of his lips were only a breath away.

"I love you, Barrett."

His response was to capture her mouth. The kiss was once again filled with an eagerness she'd never imagined possible. An illusive taste of what could be.

He ended the kiss, but lingered for several long moments with his forehead lightly resting on hers. Was it a gentle communing of souls, an effort to compose himself, or a gathering of courage?

So much depended on his next words.

"Ah, my unpredictable Casey. Life will never be the same without you."

Her spirit and her eyes stung. Her cheeks burned as if she'd been slapped. He'd given no acknowledgment of her love, no encouragement for the future. Instead he'd silenced her with a cunning tool.

His kiss.

Life will never be the same without you.

Which was lawyer-speak for life goes on and you will not be part of it.

Enough said. She'd hung her heart out there and he'd swatted it like a cheap piñata. Well, if he thought she'd fall apart like some adoring female who needed a man to pick up the broken pieces, he could think again. She turned about-face and began a determined march toward the slip where the rented sailboat waited.

"I'll work on being more predictable today," she tossed over her shoulder.

She didn't dare let him see her face, with the crimson streaks of shame snaking up her neck, inflaming her skin. She snatched off her Cowboy Cartel cap and swiped at the curls that dangled in her eyes, dabbing away tears that threatened to spill over her lashes.

"Man, it's gonna be a hot one." She fanned herself with the cap before pulling it low on her forehead. "Good thing I put on plenty of sunscreen." She buffed her palms over her cheeks as if rubbing in lotion that had been carefully applied before the mirror that morning. Her cover-up was almost complete. She slid a new pair of SeaSpecs up over her eyes and snapped the elastic band around the back of her head.

Stopping beside slip number eleven, she pretended to admire the sleek craft bobbing in the chop from the recent passing of an outboard. She was prepared to do anything to cover her gaff, to pretend her admission had been delivered with as little care and thought as Barrett had used to acknowledge it.

If they took a dunk, she'd laugh it off like a good sailor. She'd let the beauty of the sea and sky begin to heal the deep wound in her heart.

And she'd prove she could let go of the reins and let somebody else take charge if it killed her!

For the fourth time in as many days, Barrett found himself in catch-up mode with the long-legged brunette who was so bent on doing everything her way. *She* chose when and how to express her feelings. *She* made all the decisions, called all the shots. *She* had all the necessary training and credentials, so a mentor was of no value in her eyes.

And she had such a low opinion of his family craft that there seemed little he could do or say to earn her respect. Given all that, how was a man supposed to react to such a completely unexpected declaration of love? Just at the moment when he'd begun to respond, to tell her how she had impacted his life, she'd turned on her heel and stalked away with the weather apparently uppermost in her thoughts.

Casey was a conundrum, a powerhouse wrapped up in contradiction. If she'd only give him some encouragement that she could be flexible, that she was willing to bend even the slightest, that her love could be unconditional, he wouldn't have hesitated to tell her he shared her feelings.

His own imperfections were many and he'd spent years having them pointed out in professional failure upon failure. Could she be trusted to accept him as he was or would she forever be casting out a fleece, looking for verification that she'd made the right decision?

Love hadn't come into his life by decision.

Love had just shown up, in steel-toed boots and curls.

This tender emotion he felt for Casey was beyond all he'd imagined and he was going to have to take a huge risk in order to embrace it. Unlike Stanton and Colby, Barrett was deliberate and cautious to a fault. He didn't take bold chances, not with his career and certainly not with his emotions. If he told Casey how he felt, if he shared the mosaic for his future that seemed to finally be taking shape in his mind, could she stand by him? Would she agree to something untried and untrue that didn't line up with the plans she was determined to see become her reality?

"I used Google to search small-craft sailing last night so I wouldn't be a total handicap today," she announced as he stopped beside her.

Did she truly intend to gloss right over the endearing moment as if it hadn't happened? As if professing her love was something she did all the time? And as the possibility soaked into his mind, the thumping in his chest slowed. It was entirely plausible he'd misunderstood her meaning, and that friendship or a brotherly kind of love was all that she'd declared. Perhaps romantic love was something else altogether and not at all what she was experiencing toward him. He'd never known such confusion.

"Why the long face, Counselor?" she inquired. "You look as if your only client just got the death penalty."

She seemed to have no sense of the jagged gash in the core of his spirit. Either she didn't have the ability to detect his pain or she didn't care to exercise it.

"Capital punishment in the U.K. was abolished over forty years ago. Life imprisonment is the worst we have to fear."

And for the first time he had to consider what that meant. Life without the woman he loved would be no life at all. His cozy little world back home would become his prison with immediate family and unfulfilling work as the only visitors to his cell. But he couldn't build a life with a woman who refused to trust him. In the event that was to be his sentence, he'd make the most of today.

Twenty-four hours from now, memories of Casey Hardy might be his only comfort. As if she sensed his worry, she pulled off her cap, shoved her sunglasses up on her forehead and dazzled him with her smile. She let the warm morning breeze whip soft ringlets about the bluest eyes he'd ever know in this life. The precious memory was filed away for another time.

"Well, my worst fear today is how frizzy it's going to be once the humidity has its way with my mop."

"Then between the two of us we have no worries at all. Let's catch some wind."

He put one foot on the bow of the small cruiser and extended his hand to steady her as she boarded. Casey looked down at his palm to find Nemo's reassuring smile covering the last angry scrape. She accepted Barrett's grasp as she left dry land and he took it as a sign of good things to come for the day.

* * *

"Barrett, I'm sorry this morning has been such a disaster." Casey looked at her watch as if eager to get on with the second half of her day and be rid of him.

She stood idle on the dock while he coiled ropes and organized the rig.

"I've never found it so hard to help out in my life."

The lines of consternation in her face implied genuine distress, but her behavior for the past four hours had been nothing short of mutinous.

"Is that what you call it? *Helping out?*" Barrett snapped, stepping up to her level after completing his work.

Her eyes grew round with disbelief at his barely veiled accusation. He wheeled about and headed for the car, certain the stubborn little spitfire would be hot on his heels.

"Of course. I tried to do just as you told me."

"So you say." He made no effort to slow his pace. It was her turn to catch up with him. He'd seen and heard quite enough. The outcome for his final proposal was determined. There was no turning back, no need to second-guess his decision. Casey Hardy was head-strong and driven, take-charge and self-motivated. Under the right conditions she'd blossom. Under the wrong ones she'd implode.

"So you say," he repeated.

"What does that mean?" She hurried along and he lengthened his stride to keep her a half step behind.

"It means that if you'd endeavored today as I've seen you do this week, we'd have been a dynamic team out there. But because it wasn't really of interest to you, the effort on your end was mostly talk and half-hearted action."

"That's not true," she insisted. "I did everything you said."

"And nothing more. Casey, I didn't bring you here today to be a spectator. I needed to experience you as my partner, to see if you'd learn from me and to share instincts that until today appeared remarkably good. But you're so determined to be in control that even if it means following instructions poorly you'll do it because that gives you a measure of satisfaction. It makes you right when someone else is wrong."

Reaching the car, he popped open the huge trunk and tossed in his soggy deck shoes. He rounded to the passenger's side next, but she'd already yanked open the door and slid onto the leather seat.

For most of the drive she was silent. He'd intended to strike a nerve, but she was so layered and faceted, he wasn't sure his words would find the right target. He felt a moment of appreciation for Caroline's simplistic nature. Maybe that wasn't such a bad thing, after all.

"This isn't new territory for me, you know?" Casey finally spoke. "I've been hearing about my control issues all my life. But I can't help believing that having it in spades is that bad when the Bible calls it a fruit of the Spirit."

* * *

In spite of himself, laughter sprung up from inside Barrett, ringing out in the big sedan. It was the first time Casey had heard him laugh really hard. It was a beautiful sound and should have been a joyful moment. Instead it heaped a dose of embarrassment upon a deep layer of pain. They only had a few hours left together and they were arguing.

She had to admit he was right. She'd been so determined to prove everything was fine and she was all loosey-goosey with relaxation that she'd tensed up and clammed up. If he specifically asked for something outside of his reach or suggested she move left or right, she complied. She spoke when spoken to and smiled when smiled at. But otherwise she'd made no effort to share the work or to understand the dynamics of the sport. By the end of the trip it was obvious he'd have been better off sailing alone.

"Ah, I needed that." He wiped at his eyes. "I'm sorry to laugh at you, darling girl. But the fruit of the Spirit is *self-control,* using discipline and restraint to manage our willful nature. That's very different from controlling the people and situations around us so we have a sense of power over our circumstances."

"Well, it's worked for me so far."

He angled the Caddy across two empty spaces in front of her condo. He put the car in Park but left the motor running. He made it clear from their first meeting that he wasn't planning to stick around.

Not today. Not ever.

"I'm afraid it's not going to be enough this time, Casey."

"Would you like to come inside and explain that over lemonade?" Their final moments were bearing down on her and she'd blown it. Time was the one thing she needed most and she had no control over it.

"I'm afraid not. I have a quite lot of work to do before I catch my flight tomorrow. I need to finalize my recommendation and e-mail it to the board so we can discuss it Monday morning."

"It can't wait another twenty-four hours?"

"Even if I needed another day it's not an option. Sunday is Mum's birthday celebration. I can't disappoint my parents."

Of course not. He wouldn't let them down, any more than she or any of her siblings would let their parents down. It hurt all the more that, as quickly as she'd found him, she was losing the man whose focus was on his family where it belonged.

"Well, would you at least care to give me a sneak preview of the good news?"

The apologetic sadness in his eyes said it all. But he spoke the words so there would be no mistaking the facts.

"It's not the news you're hoping for, Casey. As much as I wanted this to work out in your favor, this is not the right opportunity for our client. I'm going to recommend against it. You have an astute head for business, so you must believe this short-term setback will work out for the long-term good. Please, this is an area where you're simply going to have to trust me."

Even though she was braced for it, hearing Barrett say the words struck her like brass knuckles to a glass jaw. All hope shattered as a rush of blood flooded her temples and pounded a cadence.

Trust me. Trust me. Trust me.

Two words with such power for good. But all too often they caused immeasurable destruction instead.

Ever the English gentleman even while throwing a damsel under a double-decker bus, Barrett hurried around to open her door. When she emerged into the heat she gave him a resigned smile.

"You're not angry, then?" He voiced his confusion.

"Barrett, we're adults. All's fair in love, war and business. I did my best to get into your good graces so I could sway your decision and I fell short of the mark." She gave his cheek a soft stroke with her fingertips, hoping to appear sophisticated and casual when the truth was she needed to touch him one last time.

"You were my first choice but not my only choice, so don't worry about H & H. We'll be fine."

She turned to walk away and after a few paces he called out to her.

"Wait! May I phone you? You're entitled to the final write-up and I'd like to explain it in person."

"That won't be necessary." She waved away his

offer. "But I would appreciate a signed copy by courier so I can get on with alternatives."

She reached the front door and turned for a last glance as she worked the key into the lock. He remained at the passenger's side of the car as if uncertain what to do next.

Good. Welcome to the club.

She let herself into the quiet interior, tossed her bag and keys on the coffee table, slumped down on the sofa and lifted her eyes to plead for help.

Father, I hear Your message loud and clear. This is a battle for control that I was always meant to lose. In a few short days the love of my life has come and gone and he's never likely to pass this way again. Tomorrow he'll head home to another country and another life. He's taking my dying dreams with him and leaving my battered heart and spirit behind. I need You to speak to me, Lord. Please give me some reassurance through Your word.

Determined not to cry, she filled her lungs with a deep breath and reached for her Bible. Her hand stopped, poised above the opened pages. There, beside the Proverb she'd underlined days before, lay the coin bearing the fish symbol.

The sign that Barrett could be trusted.

And now the sign that she'd be a fool to ever trust at all.

Chapter Fifteen

A week to the day after his return to England, Barrett Wesby Westbrook IV careened boldly across the Galveston job site in search of Cooper's Jeep. As white dust kicked up in the wake of his monster SUV, he put a name to the odd sensation he'd experienced since the aircraft wheels had touched down in Houston that morning.

Welcome. He felt welcome.

The return to Texas had brought the rush of comfort he couldn't find back home. Inside the walls of his London town house where he'd once enjoyed complete calm he found instead a lonely quiet. Not even his mother's birthday dinner had eased the ache or filled the emptiness. Watching the contented couples only exacerbated his profound sense of loss.

He missed Casey and there was no point pretending otherwise. Once reality had come tumbling down on him, he couldn't wrap up the thousand and one details and get back to her soon enough.

Barrett spotted one of the black Cowboy Cartel pickups and pulled alongside.

"Nice ride." Manny gave a thumbs-up to Barrett's red Hummer.

"I couldn't resist it on the rental lot," he admitted.

"All men have truck itch. It's just a matter of how big the wheels have be to scratch it." Manny gave a loving pat to the door where the double "C" logo gleamed. "I'm surprised to run into you. Heard you were back on the far side of the pond."

"That was temporary, to take care of personal matters."

At the mention of personal matters, Barrett got right to the point.

"Can you tell me where I can find Casey?"

"Gee, I haven't seen her on the site for over a week now."

A sense of dread gripped his spirit. Had she succumbed to the heebie-jeebies? Had he aided in giving her a panic attack she couldn't survive?

"Check over at the trailer. Savannah and Cooper were there when I dropped by earlier," Manny suggested.

"Thanks, mate."

Barrett ground the gears as he followed the diagram on the knob and wrestled the stick into place.

"And don't be a stranger! Let's wet a hook soon!"

Manny called as his window slid up in anticipation of the inevitable swirl of dust.

Relief surged at the sight of Cooper's Wrangler outside the construction office. News of Casey was only moments away. Surprisingly though, all was quiet when he let himself through the door.

"Cheers! Anybody here?" he called.

"Barrett?" Surprise was evident in Savannah's voice as she emerged from the conference room and immediately offered a hug.

"Howdy, stranger." Cooper was right behind her, his hand outstretched in friendship.

A lump of gratitude for their hospitality thickened Barrett's throat. As much as he wanted to explore the sensation, he needed word of his beloved much more. He made no effort to disguise his glance around the room for a sign of her presence.

"She's not here." Savannah answered the unspoken question. "She hasn't been back into the office since you left."

"Is she ill? Did she have another attack?" The quickening in his chest said he would be ill himself if he didn't find her soon.

Savannah looked to Cooper who nodded his head, giving agreement to speak freely.

"No, that's the cool part of all this. What should have sent her over the edge gave her a breakthrough. She absolutely refused to succumb to despair. She got into the Word and kept insisting she would simply trust."

Thank You, Father! She'd held on to trust, after all. But would she ever trust him again?

"So she's fine, then." Barrett felt mild relief.

"I didn't say that. Don't console yourself thinking she hasn't had a rough week, Barrett. You threw our girl a curve ball, but she pulled out of the funk and made a conscious decision to find something positive in the pain."

He cringed inside. He'd caused her pain on so many levels and then left her to deal with it alone. Would she listen to his reasons? Would she forgive him?

Would she still love him?

Warm fingers rested on his arm and Savannah's eyes glistened with compassion.

"Honey, she's taken some time off to get a fresh perspective. In that strange way that God unfolds His plan, the wake-up call you gave her was just what she needed. It forced her to take a look at her life and reconsider the collision course she was on."

"She phones me daily for a progress report but otherwise she's letting me do my job like she should have from the beginning." Cooper spoke up.

"Has she left Texas?" Barrett held his breath for the answer, never having considered that she wouldn't be there when he returned. He'd been such a fool, making judgments and drawing conclusions with only half the evidence. Ironic, but further confirmation his personal decision had been spot-on, after all.

"No way, dubs! She may have agreed to ease up but

abdicate is not in that little lady's vocabulary." Cooper chuckled and turned aside to spit discreetly into his cup.

"She's at the marina," Savannah offered as she checked her watch. "You should be able to find her at slip number eleven unless she's finished up already. You'd better hurry before she gets away."

"I guarantee you this. If she gives me any say in the matter that will never happen again."

The trip to the oceanfront was endless as he considered what to say, what to do. With practiced words on his lips, he proudly tugged the new Stetson low on his brow and bounded across the parking lot, onto the boardwalk and around the water's edge. At the sight of Casey his lungs deflated, his heart sunk low in his chest and his feet refused to carry him the final twenty-five meters.

She was laughing, happy in a way he hadn't witnessed in their days together. Her enchanting curls were blowing free with only her fancy new sailing shades as a headband. With one knee pressed to the dock for support she expertly coiled a rope at her feet.

While she worked, she gave all her attention to a tanned and well-built man standing beside her who had to be fifteen years Barrett's junior. He recalled the recent number on his bathroom scale and sucked in his stomach.

Oh, not again.

He'd put the situation with Caroline behind him

forever. Was it going to resurrect itself in the form of another younger man willing to make a sacrifice he wouldn't?

Sacrifice?

An insane way to think of love. What he wouldn't truly sacrifice to have Casey gaze at him as she was looking at another man this very moment! To have her repeat the words he'd heard her say the first time and shamelessly made her repeat. And now he longed with all his soul to witness the declaration again.

Please, Father, let all the steps of my life be leading to this moment. Let this love be Your will!

Casey gave a fond look at her little cruiser before making a final check of the bow line. Satisfied it was securely bound to the cleat, she reached for Chip's hand and let him help her to her feet. As he'd done for the past four days, the young instructor draped his arm around her shoulders to give her a quick squeeze of reassurance.

"Nice work today. See you tomorrow," he confirmed before heading for his next appointment.

She hoisted her small backpack, slung it over her shoulder and turned to leave before she spotted him. The moment of intense déjà vu made her soul cry out. It also produced the high-pitched shriek usually reserved for rodent sightings.

No farther than thirty yards away stood a man in a straw cowboy hat who was either Barrett Westbrook or Hugh Grant. Either way, he was about to have a woman in his arms. She dropped the bag filled with soggy towels, met him somewhere in the middle and flung herself into his embrace.

"Oh, I'm so glad to see you!" She pressed her face to his chest, breathed in his scent and pulled him tight. The drumming of his heart was the sweetest music ever.

Trust me, trust me, trust me, it insisted.

It was the same message the Holy Spirit had given her during her study. Over and over, God revealed Himself to her as she dug deeper into His Word for comfort. He recalled to her the Proverb of committing plans to Him so they would succeed. And she'd not only rededicated her plans, she'd laid her very life at His feet and pleaded for His mercy and guidance in every area. She had no idea what the future held, but she was certain He had a plan infinitely better than anything she'd devised on her own.

"Thank God you still feel that way," he muttered into her hair, wild from the morning sail.

Not only was her hair out of control, she knew she was dressed like a freak in colors that didn't match and worn-out old sneakers that nobody but family should see. But he didn't seem to notice as he stared down into her face, his slate-gray eyes brimming, about to spill over.

As one corner leaked a fat tear, she brushed it away tenderly.

"Hey, I know the news you brought me is bad, but you look like you just lost your best friend."

"I hope with all my might that's not the case."

He placed a chaste kiss on the tip of her nose, then took her hand and led her to a shady bench nearby. Tugging her down to sit close beside him, he held fast to her hand.

"Speaking of friends, who was yours?" He nodded in the direction Chip had walked.

She smiled at the question. Proud of the answer. But mostly adoring the proper cowboy before her.

"Chip is my coach. He's teaching me to sail my new boat."

She pointed toward the fifteen-foot *Montgomery* bobbing in the water of slip eleven. The same one they'd shared during their dreadful sailing experience together.

"I had to learn on something and since you hand-picked her for the day, I figured she was a good choice to buy. My brother's been after me for years to put money into something besides designer shoes, so there's my start. What do you think?"

"As I said last week, your unpredictable nature has changed my life. But I had no idea how completely and for the better all the changes would be."

She wanted to take his comforting closeness and his sweet words as good signs but there had to be much, much more. There had to be a chance he could love her totally, warts and all. She'd put everything at risk when she'd shared her heart. His lack of response had nearly crippled her. God's healing touch had kept her from sinking and had set her feet on solid ground. But she wouldn't jump into the deep again for less than she deserved.

For less than the one man who would cherish her forever.

"Tell me about these changes," she encouraged while silently praying for strength to accept whatever he had to say.

"Let me start with the outcome of my investigation."

"Oh, that." She pulled her hand out of Barrett's. "You didn't need to come thousands of miles when I told you a courier would be fine with me."

He scooped her hand back between his and held it securely.

"You're in no position to accept 'fine' ever again, Casey. Your communication requirements will take a significant leap now that you're to be the U.S. point for an international partnership."

She twisted on the bench to look him full in the face.

"But I thought you were going to recommend against it. Against me."

The words were a knife shoved deeper into still-fresh wounds. The sadness in Barrett's eyes said the wounds were his, as well. That he'd suffered as she had.

"I did, my darling. My opening statement said you were not yet prepared to take on the role. But the facts and anecdotes I presented during the argument completely enchanted the client. They want a maverick. They want you, Casey. This isn't even about Hearth and Home anymore. It's about you. As my last official act for Westbrook Partners, Esquire, I've come to deliver a contract for your consideration."

She pulled her hands free to cover her eyes.

"This can't be happening. I've spent a week accepting defeat, reconsidering my life goals, deciding what I want to do next. Journaling about new personal challenges I want to take on. Even thinking about nonprofit work."

He pulled her hands away and lowered his face to hers. The curve of his lips and the squint of his eyes melted her worries. None of that mattered. It could all wait. Barrett was here, now.

And she loved him with all her might.

She sat upright. "Hold the phone. What was that you said about your last official act?"

"I resigned."

"You what?" She might have been losing control but he'd lost his senses!

"I resigned. Casey, this assignment wasn't simply another effort to find my role with the firm, it was my final option. There's nothing left for me to try. I put my heart into this experience. I presented my best case and the client voted against me. Quiet honestly, I stink at every facet of the family practice and I'm not going to invest another moment of my life where it's never going to bear fruit. I broke the news to my parents two days ago and they not only accepted my decision, they blessed it. They think it's high time I get on with something fulfilling, and more importantly, begin an official period of courtship."

And she'd thought the worst was over!

Father God, please let me get through this conversation and away from this place before I lose it. Shock and grief are beginning to run together in my mind. Help me, Father!

She looked down at her hands. They were steady, there was no tingling, no shaking, and though her heart raced, it was due to the nearness of the man, not the imminence of a collapse. She would recover from this new pain. In time.

"So, you're going to have that old-fashioned courtship you talked about." Her voice was calm, steady.

"Actually…" He eased off the bench and down onto one knee. She thought for a moment he must have dropped something. But instead of searching the grass, he looked into her eyes, his own once again bright with emotion.

"Actually, I was hoping for a Lone Star courtship. With my sweet American girl. With my unpredictable and wonderful Casey."

"Are you saying you love me?" Her voice crescendoed, incredulous. Her sisters would howl at the stupid question, but she had to hear him say it.

"Of course I do. But those words are not sufficient

to tell you how I feel. I adore you. I treasure you. My life will never be the same without you. I want you for my bride. Please say you'll marry me."

She leaned forward, brushed her lips to his, and their tears mingled where cheek pressed to cheek.

"What about your work?"

He pulled back to look into her face. The love she saw mirrored there was a flood of joy in her heart. Her vision blurred.

"My work will be with you if you'll agree to be my first client. Whether you believe it or not, you are going to need a business coach and I'm the *only* man for the job. I may eventually decide to hang out my shingle for that purpose, but there's no rush."

"What about your home, your family?"

He cupped warm hands around her face and brushed away tears. God had replaced the dreams of a girl with His plan for a man and a woman.

His perfect plan that would succeed.

"Wherever you go, I will go with you. We can stay in Texas, go back to Iowa, travel the world. You may be in control of that decision if it pleases you. We have a lifetime to decide. There will be ample opportunity for me to take my precious Casey to my family home and my magical Tintagel."

He drew her close and just before their lips met he whispered words from his soul to hers.

"I love you, Casey. With you beside me, any place on earth will be our Camelot."

Dear Reader,

You've probably heard the saying that there is a God-shaped hole in your heart that only He can fill. But have you ever considered the opposite is true? There is a void in God's heart that will only be satisfied by you. Our Father created us to desire relationships with others but more importantly to seek after an everlasting bond with Him. He misses you when you're too busy to hear His voice. He searches for you when you are lost in the pressures of the day. He hears when you call out in distress and He's always prepared to meet you where you are.

We live lives that are ten pounds of sugar in a five-pound sack. Eventually our seams will burst from the pressure if we allow the most important relationship of all to suffer. Don't wait for a crisis that forces you to bend your knee, be still and allow God to take control. Go to Him today with praise for the promise that all things work together for those who love Him and are called according to His purpose.

Until we meet again, let your light shine.

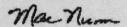

QUESTIONS FOR DISCUSSION

1. The cultural differences between Casey and Barrett might have been a problem in their relationship. Is culture something that can be overcome as long as there is other common ground? Why or why not?

2. In addition to culture there was also a significant geographic barrier between our two lovebirds. How do people in love overcome distance? How do they overcome the distance between their families?

3. Casey and Barrett were both Christians, but we do not know if they worshipped in the same denomination. As a relationship develops, when is it appropriate to have that conversation?

4. When it becomes clear that there are major differences in theology, do you give up on the relationship or pray for change? How would you counsel your sibling, best friend or child in this situation?

5. Many times couples marry without having the serious discussions identified in our first few

questions. Why do you think we avoid topics that will be so critical to the success of a committed relationship?

6. Casey is a woman I can identify with because of her driven nature. Knowing when it's time to ease up on the accelerator is a struggle for me just like it was for Casey. Do you think we've become a nation of superwomen who equate boundaries with failure? Why or why not?

7. Learning to accept and live within our limitations and/or boundaries can produce great character growth. Can you think of a time in your life when discovering a limitation actually set you free?

8. Barrett had spent almost forty years trying to fit into the family's expectations for his career. Which involves the greater risk: following the road map you've been given or striking out to find your dream? Which is more rewarding? Why or why not?

9. Discuss a time when you went against everyone else's expectations in order to create your own happiness. What happened as a result?

10. Casey and Barrett were fortunate to have dear friends in whom they could confide and seek

guidance. Why is it so difficult to have that same honesty and trust with family members who are otherwise supportive and loving?

11. Barrett's desire for a courtship period was an old-fashioned notion that appealed to Casey. Why do you think our modern world has abandoned a chaste time of personal discovery before marriage?

12. The anxiety (panic) disorder Casey experienced is the fastest growing mental diagnosis in America. She found healing through prayer. Have you or a loved one suffered from similar symptoms? How did prayer help you through your experiences?

Love Inspired™

THE McKASLIN CLAN

After a near-fatal injury in the line of duty, Jonas Lowell wakes up and can't remember his family. His loving wife Danielle tries everything to spark his memory. But with a lot of faith and a new courtship, Jonas might just fall in love all over again.

Look for

Her Wedding Wish

by

Jillian Hart

*Available June 2008
wherever you buy books.*

Steeple
Hill®

www.SteepleHill.com

LI87483

Love Inspired HISTORICAL

INSPIRATIONAL HISTORICAL ROMANCE

Arizona, 1882: Saloon owner Jake Scully knows his rough frontier town is no place for delicate Lacey Stewart. Now, ten years later, Lacey is a grown woman who deserves a respectable man, not a jaded rogue like Jake. But Jake's "delicate lady" had a mind of her own....

Look for

THE REDEMPTION OF JAKE SCULLY

by *New York Times* bestselling author

ELAINE BARBIERI

*Available June 2008
wherever you buy books.*

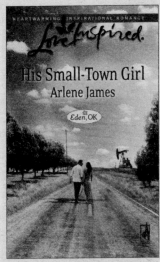

Texas CEO Tyler Aldrich believes there is nothing worse than being stuck in rural Eden, Oklahoma. Yet when he meets quiet Charlotte Jefford, something makes him want to stick around—and it isn't just her meat loaf! Have they been thrown together by a wrong turn, or has God set them on the right path?

Look for

His Small-Town Girl

by

Arlene James

Available in June wherever you buy books.

Steeple
Hill®

REQUEST YOUR FREE BOOKS!

2 FREE INSPIRATIONAL NOVELS
PLUS 2
FREE
MYSTERY GIFTS

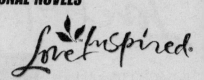

YES! Please send me 2 FREE Love Inspired® novels and my 2 FREE mystery gifts (gifts are worth about $10). After receiving them, if I don't wish to receive any more books, I can return the shipping statement marked "cancel". If I don't cancel, I will receive 4 brand-new novels every month and be billed just $4.24 per book in the U.S. or $4.74 per book in Canada, plus 25¢ shipping and handling per book and applicable taxes, if any*. That's a savings of over 20% off the cover price! I understand that accepting the 2 free books and gifts places me under no obligation to buy anything. I can always return a shipment and cancel at any time. Even if I never buy another book, the two free books and gifts are mine to keep forever.

113 IDN ERXA 313 IDN ERWX

Name _____ (PLEASE PRINT)

Address _____ Apt. #

City _____ State/Prov. _____ Zip/Postal Code

Signature (if under 18, a parent or guardian must sign)

Order online at www.LoveInspiredBooks.com

Or mail to Steeple Hill Reader Service:

IN U.S.A.: P.O. Box 1867, Buffalo, NY 14240-1867
IN CANADA: P.O. Box 609, Fort Erie, Ontario L2A 5X3

Not valid to current subscribers of Love Inspired books.

Want to try two free books from another series?
Call 1-800-873-8635 or visit www.morefreebooks.com